ULLR UPRISING

ULLR UPRISING

by H. Beam Piper

"The heathen geeks, they wear no breeks," the Terrans sang. But on a crazy world like Ullr, clothes didn't make the fighting man. There both red and yellow meant danger—and blood!

I

The big armor-tender vibrated, gently and not unpleasantly, as the contragravity field alternated on and off. Sometimes it rocked slightly, like a boat on the water, and, in the big screen which served in lieu of a window at the front of the control-cabin, the dingy-yellow landscape would seem to tilt a little. The air was faintly yellow, the sky was yellow with a greenish cast, and the clouds were green-gray.

No human had ever set foot on the surface, or breathed the air, of Niflheim. To have done so would have been instant death; the air was a mixture of free fluorine and fluoride gasses, the soil was metallic fluorides, damp with acid rains, and the river was pure hydrofluoric acid. Even the ordinary spacesuit would have been no protection; the glass and rubber and plastic would have disintegrated in a matter of minutes. People came to Niflheim, and worked the mines and uranium refineries and chemical plants, but they did so inside power-driven and contragravity-lifted armor, and they lived on artificial satellites two thousand miles off-planet. Niflheim was worse than airless; much worse.

The chief engineer sat at his controls, making the minor lateral adjustments in the vehicle's position which were not possible to the automatic controls. At his own panel of instruments, a small man with grizzled black hair around a bald crown, and a grizzled beard, chewed nervously at the stump of a dead cigar and listened intently. A large, plump-faced, young man in soiled khaki shirt and shorts, with extremely hairy legs, was doodling on his notepad and eating candy out of a bag. And a black-haired girl in a suit of coveralls three sizes too big for her, and, apparently, not much of anything else, lounged with one knee hooked over her chair-arm, staring into the screen at the distant horizon.

"I can see them," the girl said, lifting a hand in front of her. "At two o'clock, about one of my hand's-breaths above the horizon. But only four of them."

The man with the grizzled beard put his face into the fur around the eyepiece of the telescopic-'visor and twisted a dial. "You have good eyes,

5

Miss Quinton," he complimented. "The fifth's inside the handling machine. One of the Ullrans. Gorkrink."

*

The largest of the specks that had appeared on the horizon resolved itself into a handling-machine, a thing like an oversized contragravity-tank, with a bull-dozer-blade, a stubby derrick-boom instead of a gun, and jointed, claw-tipped, arms at the sides. The smaller dots grew into personal armor—egg-shaped things that sprouted arms and grab-hooks and pushers in all directions. The man with the grizzled beard began talking rapidly into his hand-phone, then hung it up. There was a series of bumps, and the armor-tender, weightless on contragravity, shook as the handling-machine came aboard.

"You ever see any nuclear bombing, Miss Quinton?" the young man with the hairy legs asked, offering her his candybag.

"Only by telecast, back Solside," Paula Quinton replied, helping herself. "Test-shots at the Federation Navy proving-ground on Mars. I never even heard of nuclear bombs being used for mining till I came here, though."

"It'll be something to see," he promised. "These volcanoes have been dormant for, oh, maybe as long as a thousand years; there ought to be a pretty good head of gas down there. The volcanoes we shot three months ago yielded a fine flow of lava with all sorts of metals—nickel, beryllium, vanadium, chromium, iridium, as well as copper and iron."

"What sort of gas were you speaking about?" she asked.

"Hydrogen. That's what's going to make the fireworks; it combines explosively with fluorine. The hydrogen-fluorine combination is what passes for combustion here: the result is hydrofluoric acid, the local equivalent of water. The subsurface hydrogen is produced when the acid filters down through the rock, combines with pure metals underneath."

The door at the rear of the control-cabin opened, and Juan Murillo, the seismologist, entered, followed by an assistant, who was not human. He was a biped, vaguely humanoid, but he had four arms and a face like a lizard's, and, except for some equipment on belt, he was entirely naked.

He spoke rapidly to Murillo, in a squeaking jabber. Murillo turned.

"Yes, if you wish, Gorkrink," he said, in Lingua Terra. Then he turned back to Gomes as the Ullran sat down in a chair by the door.

"Well, she's all yours, Lourenço; shoot the works."

Gomes stabbed the radio-detonator button in front of him.

*

Out on the rolling skyline, fifty miles away, a lancelike ray of blue-white light shot up into the gathering dusk—a clump of five rays, really, from five deep shafts in an irregular pentagon half a mile across, blended into one by the distance. An instant later, there was a blinding flash, like sheet-lightning, and a huge ball of varicolored fire belched upward, leaving a series of smoke-rings to float more slowly after it. The fireball flattened, then spread to form the mushroom-head of a column of incandescent gas that mounted to overtake it, engorging the smoke-rings as it rose, twisting, writhing, changing shape, turning to dark smoke in one moment and belching flame and crackling with lightning the next.

"In about half an hour," the large young man told Paula Quinton, "the real fireworks should be starting. What's coming up now is just small debris from the nuclear blast. When the shock-waves get down far enough to crack things open, the gas'll come up, and then steam and ash, and then magma."

"Well, even this was worth staying over for," the girl said, watching the screen.

"You going on to Ullr on the *City of Canberra?*" Lourenço Gomes asked. "I wish I were; I have to stay over and make another shot, in a month or so, and I've had about all of Niflheim I can take, now."

"When are you going to Terra?" the girl asked him.

"Terra? I don't know; a year, two years. But I'm going to Ullr on the next ship—the *City of Pretoria*—if we get the next blast off in time. They want me to design some improvements on a couple of power-reactors at Keegark so I'll probably see you when I get there."

"Here she comes!" the chief engineer called. "Watch the base of the column!"

The pillar of fiery smoke and dust, still boiling up from where the bombs had gone off far underground, was being violently agitated at the bottom. A series of new flashes broke out, lifting and spreading the incandescent radioactive gasses, and then a great gush of flame rose. A column of pure hydrogen must have rushed up into the vacuum created by the explosion; the next blast of flame, in a lateral sheet, came at nearly ten thousand feet above the ground. Then geysers of hot ash and molten rock spouted upward; some of the white-hot debris landed almost at the acid river, half-way to the armor-tender.

"We've started a first-class earthquake, too," Murillo said, looking at the instruments.

"About six big cracks opening in the rock-structure. You know, when this quiets down and cools off, we'll have more ore on the surface than we can handle in ten years, and more than we could have mined by ordinary means in fifty."

"Well, that finishes our work," the large young man said, going to a kit-bag in the corner of the cabin and getting out a bottle. "Get some of those plastic cups, over there, somebody; this one calls for a drink."

The Ullran, in the background, rose quickly and squeaked apologetically. Murillo nodded. "Yes, of course, Gorkrink. No need for you to stay here." The Ullran went out, closing the door behind him.

"That taboo against Ullrans and Terrans watching each other eat and drink," Paula Quinton commented. "But you were speaking to him in Lingua Terra; I didn't know any of them understood it."

"Gorkrink does," Murillo said, uncorking the bottle and pouring into the plastic cups. "None of them can speak it, of course, because of the structure of their vocal organs, any more than we can speak their languages without artificial aids. But I can talk to him in Lingua Terra without having to put one of those damn gags in my mouth, and he can pass my instructions on to the others. He's been a big help; I'll be sorry to lose him."

"Lose him?"

"Yes, his year's up; he's going back to Ullr on the *Canberra*. He's from Keegark; claims to be a prince, or something. But he's a damn good worker. Very smart; picks things up the first time you tell him. I'll recommend him unqualifiedly for any kind of work with contragravity or mechanized equipment."

They all had drinks, now, except the chief engineer, who wanted a rain-check on his.

"Well, here's to us," Murillo said. "The first A-bomb miners in history...."

II

H. BEAM PIPER

Carlos von Schlichten, General of the troops on Ullr, threw his cigarette away and set his monocle more firmly in his eye, stepping forward to let Brigadier-General Themistocles M'zangwe and little Colonel Hideyoshi O'Leary follow him out of the fort. On the little hundred-foot-square parade ground in front of the keep, his aircar was parked, and the soldiers were assembled.

Ten or twelve of them were Terrans—a couple of lieutenants, sergeants, gunners, technicians, the sergeant-driver and corporal-gunner of his own car. The other fifty-odd were Ullrans. They stood erect on stumpy legs and broad, six-toed feet. They had four arms apiece, one pair from true shoulders and the other connected to a pseudo-pelvis midway down the torso. Their skins were slate-gray and rubbery, speckled with pinhead-sized bits of quartz that had been formed from perspiration, since their body-tissues were silicone instead of carbon-hydrogen. Their narrow heads were unpleasantly saurian; they had small, double-lidded red eyes, and slit-like nostrils, and wide mouths filled with opalescent teeth. Being cold-blooded, they needed no clothing, beyond their belts and equipment, and the emblem of the Chartered Ullr Company painted on their chests and backs. They had no need for modesty, since all were of the same gender—true, functional hermaphrodites; any individual among them could bear young, or fertilize the ova of any other individual.

Fifteen years before, when he had come to Ullr as a newly commissioned colonel in the army of the Ullr Company, it had taken him some time to adjust. But now his mind disregarded them and went on worrying about the mysterious disappearance of pet animals from Terran homes; there must be some connection with the subtle change he had noticed in the attitudes of the natives, but he couldn't guess what. He didn't like it, though, any more than the beginning of cannibalism among the wild Jeel tribesmen. Or the visit of Paula Quinton on Ullr as field-agent for the Extraterrestrials' Rights Association; now was no time to stir up trouble among the natives, unless his hunch was wrong.

He shrugged it aside and climbed into the command-car, followed by M'zangwe and O'Leary. Sergeant Harry Quong and Corporal Hassan Bogdanoff took their places in the front seat; the car lifted, turned to nose into the wind, and rose in a slow spiral.

"Where now, sir?" Quong asked.

ULLR UPRISING

"Back to Konkrook; to the island."

*

The nose of the car swung east by south; the cold-jet rotors began humming, and the hot-jets were cut in. The car turned from the fort and the mountains and shot away over the foothills toward the coastal plains. Below were forests, yellow-green with new foliage of the second growing-season of the equatorial year, veined with narrow dirt roads and spotted with occasional clearings. Farther east, the dirty gray woodsmoke of Ullr marked the progress of the charcoal-burnings. That was the only natural fuel on Ullr; there was too much silica on Ullr and not enough of anything else; what would be coal-seams on Terra were strata of silicified wood. And, of course, there was no petroleum. There was less charcoal being burned now than formerly; the Ullr Company had been bringing in great quantities of synthetic thermoconcentrate-fuel, and had been setting up nuclear furnaces and nuclear-electric power-plants, wherever they gained a foothold on the planet.

As planets went, Ullr was no bargain, he thought sourly. At times, he wished he had never followed the lure of rapid promotion and fanatically high pay and left the Federation regulars for the army of the Ullr Company. If he hadn't, he'd probably be a colonel, at five thousand sols a year, but maybe it would be better to be a middle-aged colonel on a decent planet than a Company army general at twenty-five thousand on this combination icebox, furnace, wind-tunnel and stonepile, where the water tasted like soapsuds and left a crackly film when it dried; where the temperature ranged, from pole to pole, between two hundred and fifty and minus a hundred and fifty Fahrenheit and the Beaufort-scale ran up to thirty; where nothing that ran or swam or grew was fit for a human to eat.

Ahead, the city of Konkrook sprawled along the delta of the Konk river and extended itself inland. The river was dry, now. Except in Spring, when it was a red-brown torrent, it never ran more than a trickle, and not at all this late in the Northern Summer. The aircar lost altitude, and the hot-jet stopped firing. They came gliding in over the suburbs and the yellow-green parks, over the low one-story dwellings and shops, the lofty temples and palaces, the fantastically-twisted towers, following a street that became increasingly mean and squalid as it neared the industrial district along the waterfront.

H. BEAM PIPER

*

Von Schlichten, on the right, glanced idly down, puffing slowly on his cigarette. Then he stiffened, the muscles around his right eye clamping tighter on the monocle. Leaning forward, he punched Harry Quong lightly on the man's right shoulder.

"Yes, sir; I saw it," the Chinese-Australian driver replied. "Terrans in trouble; bein' mobbed by geeks. Aircar parked right in the bloody middle of it."

The car made a twisting, banking loop and came back, more slowly. Von Schlichten had the handset of the car's radio, and was punching out the combination of the Company guardhouse on Gongonk Island; he held down the signal button until he got an answer.

"Von Schlichten, in car over Konkrook. Riot on Fourth Avenue, just off Seventy-second Street." No Terran could possibly remember the names of Konkrook's streets; even native troops recruited from outside found the numbers easier to learn and remember. "Geeks mobbing a couple of Terrans. I'm going down, now, to do what I can to help; send troops in a hurry. Kragan Rifles. And stand by; my driver'll give it to you as it happens."

The voice of somebody at the guardhouse, bawling orders, came out of the receiver as he tossed the phone forward over Harry Quong's shoulder; Quong caught it and began speaking rapidly and urgently into it while he steered with the other hand. Von Schlichten took one of the five-pound spiked riot-maces out of the rack in front of him.

Bogdanoff rose into the ball-turret and swung the twin 15-mm.'s around, cutting loose. Quong brought the car in fast, at about shoulder-height on the mob. Between them, they left a swath of mangled, killed, wounded, and stunned natives. Then, spinning the car around, Quong set it down hard on a clump of rioters as close as possible to the struggling group around the two Terrans. Von Schlichten threw back the canopy and jumped out of the car, O'Leary and M'zangwe behind him.

There was another aircar, a dark maroon civilian job, at the curb; its native driver was slumped forward over the controls, a short crossbow-bolt sticking out of his neck. Backed against the closed door of a house, a Terran with white hair and a small beard was clubbing futilely with an empty pistol. He was wounded, and blood was streaming over his face. His

11

companion, a young woman in a long fur coat, was laying about her with a native bolo-knife.

*

Von Schlichten's mace had a spiked ball-head, and a four-inch spike in front of that. He smashed the ball down on the back of one Ullran's head, and jabbed another in the rump with the spike.

"*Zak! Zak!*" he yelled, in pidgin-Ullran. "*Jik-jik*, you lizard-faced Creator's blunder!"

The Ullran whirled, swinging a blade somewhere between a big butcher-knife and a small machete. His mouth was open, and there was froth on his lips.

"*Znidd suddabit!*" he shrieked.

Von Schlichten parried the cut on the steel shaft of his mace. "*Suddabit* yourself!" he shouted back, ramming the spike-end into the opal-filled mouth. "And *znidd* you, too," he added, recovering and slamming the ball-head down on the narrow saurian skull. The Ullran went down, spurting a yellow fluid about the consistency of gun-oil.

Ahead, one of the natives had caught the wounded Terran with both lower hands, and was raising a dagger with his upper right. The girl in the fur coat swung wildly, slashing the knife-arm, then chopped down on the creature's neck.

Another of them closed with the girl, grabbing her right arm with all four hands and biting at her; she screamed and kicked her attacker in the groin, where an Ullran is, if anything, even more vulnerable than a Terran. The native howled hideously, and von Schlichten, jumping over a couple of corpses, shoved the muzzle of his pistol into the creature's open mouth and pulled the trigger, blowing its head apart like a rotten pumpkin and splashing both himself and the girl with yellow blood and rancid-looking gray-green brains.

O'Leary, jumping forward after von Schlichten, stuck his dagger into the neck of a rioter and left it there, then caught the girl around the waist with his free arm. M'zangwe dropped his mace and swung the frail-looking man onto his back. Together, they struggled back to the command-car, von Schlichten covering the retreat with his pistol. Another rioter was aiming one of the long-barreled native air-rifles, holding the ten-inch globe of the air-chamber in both lower hands. Von Schlichten shot him, and the native literally blew to pieces.

For an instant, he wondered how the small bursting-charge of a 10-mm. explosive pistol-bullet could accomplish such havoc, and assumed that the native had been carrying a bomb in his belt. Then another explosion tossed fragmentary corpses nearby, and another and another. Glancing quickly over his shoulder, he saw four combat-cars coming in, firing with 40-mm. auto-cannon and 15-mm. machine-guns. They swept between the hovels on one side and the warehouses on the other, strafing the mob, darted up to a thousand feet, looped, and came swooping back, and this time there were three long blue-gray troop-carriers behind them.

These landed in the hastily-cleared street and began disgorging native Company soldiers—Kragan mercenaries, he noted with satisfaction. They carried a modified version of the regular Terran Federation infantry rifle, stocked and sighted to conform to their physical peculiarities, with long, thorn-like, triangular bayonets. One platoon ran forward, dropped to one knee, and began firing rapidly into what was left of the mob. Four-handed soldiers can deliver a simply astonishing volume of fire, particularly when armed with auto-rifles having twenty-shot drop-out magazines which can be changed with the lower hands without lowering the weapon.

*

There was a clatter of shod hoofs, and a company of King Jaikark of Konkrook's cavalry came trotting up on their six-legged, lizard-headed, quartz-speckled, mounts. Some of these charged into side alleys, joyfully lancing and cutting-down fleeing rioters, while others dismounted, three tossing their reins to a fourth, and went to work with their crossbows. Von Schlichten, who ordinarily entertained a dim opinion of the King of Konkrook's soldiery, admitted, grudgingly, that it was smart work; four hands were a big help in using a crossbow, too.

A Terran captain of native infantry came over, saluting.

"Are you and your people all right, general?" he asked.

Von Schlichten glanced at the front seat of his car, where Harry Quong, a pistol in his right hand, was still talking into the radio-phone, and Hassan Bogdanoff was putting fresh belts into his guns. Then he saw that they had gotten the wounded man into the car. The girl, having dropped her bolo, was leaning against the side of the car.

"We seem to be, Captain Pedolsky. Very smart work; you must have those vehicles of yours on hyperspace-drive.... How is he, colonel?"

"We'd better get him to the hospital, right away," O'Leary replied. "I think he has a concussion."

"Harry, call the hospital. Tell them what the score is, and tell them we're bringing the casualty in to their top landing stage.... Why, we'll make out very nicely, captain. You'd better stay around with your Kragans and make sure that these geeks of King Jaikark's don't let the riot flare up again and get away from them. And don't let them get the impression that they can maintain order around here without our help; the Company would like to see that attitude discouraged."

"Yes, sir; I understand." Captain Pedolsky opened the pouch on his belt and took out the false palate and tongue-clicker without which no Terran could do more than mouth a crude and barely comprehensible pidgin-Ullran. Stuffing the gadget into his mouth, he turned and began jabbering orders.

Von Schlichten helped the girl into the car, placing her on his right. The wounded civilian was propped up in the left corner of the seat, and Colonel O'Leary and Brigadier-General M'zangwe took the jump-seats. The driver put on the contragravity-field, and the car lifted up.

"Them, see if there's a flask and a drinking-cup in the door pocket next you," he said. "I think Miss Quinton could use a drink."

*

The girl turned. Even in her present disheveled condition, she was beautiful—a trifle on the petite side, with black hair and black eyes that quirled up oddly at the outer corners. Her nails were black-lacquered and spotted with little gold stars, evidently a new feminine fad from Terra.

"I certainly could, general.... How did you know my name?"

"You've been on Ullr for the last three months; ever since the *City of Canberra* got in from Niflheim. On Ullr, there aren't enough of us that everybody doesn't know all about everybody else. You're Dr. Paula Quinton; you're an extraterrestrial sociographer, and you're a field-agent for the Extraterrestrials' Rights Association, like Mohammed Ferriera, here." He took the cup and flask from Themistocles M'zangwe and poured her a drink. "Take this easy, now; Baldur honey-rum, a hundred and fifty proof."

He watched her sip the stuff cautiously, cough over the first mouthful, and then get the rest of it down.

"More?" When she shook her head, he stoppered the flask and relieved her of the cup. "What were you doing in that district, anyhow?" he wanted to know. "I'd have thought Mohammed Ferriera would have had more sense than to take you there, or go there, himself, for that matter," he added quickly.

"We went to visit a friend of his, a native named Keeluk, who seems to be a sort of combination clergyman and labor-leader," she replied. "I'm going to observe labor conditions at the North Pole mines in a short while, and Mr. Keeluk was going to give me letters of introduction to friends of his at Skilk. We talked with Mr. Keeluk for a while, and when we came out, we found that our driver had been killed and a mob had gathered. Of course, we were carrying pistols; they're part of this survival-kit you make everybody carry, along with the emergency-rations and the water desilicator. Mr. Ferriera's wasn't loaded, but mine was. When they rushed us, I shot a couple of them, and then picked up that big knife.... I never in my life saw anything as beautiful as you coming through that mob swinging that warclub!"

*

The aircar swung out over Konkrook Channel and headed toward the blue-gray Company buildings on Gongonk Island, and the Company airport.

"Just what happened, while you and Mr. Ferriera were in Keeluk's house, Miss Quinton?" O'Leary asked, trying not to sound official. "Was Keeluk with you all the time? Or did he go out for a while, say fifteen or twenty minutes before you left?"

"Why, yes, he did." Paula Quinton looked surprised. "How did you guess it? You see, a dog started barking, behind the house, and he excused himself and...."

"A dog?" von Schlichten almost shouted. The other officers echoed him.

"Why, yes...." Paula Quinton's eyes widened. "But there are no dogs on Ullr, except a few owned by Terrans. And wasn't there something about ...?"

Von Schlichten had the radio-phone and was calling the command car at the scene of the riot. The sergeant-driver answered.

"Von Schlichten here; my compliments to Captain Pedolsky, and tell him he's to make immediate and thorough search of the house in front of which the incident occurred, and adjoining houses. For his information, that's Keeluk's house. Tell him to look for traces of Governor-General Harrington's collie, or any of the other terrestrial animals that have been disappearing—that goat, for instance, or those rabbits. And I want Keeluk brought in, alive and in condition to be interrogated."

"But, what ...?" the girl began, her voice puzzled.

"That's why you were attacked," he told her. "Keeluk was afraid to let you get away from there alive to report hearing that dog, so he went out and had a gang of thugs rounded up to kill you."

"But he was only gone five minutes."

"In five minutes, I can put all the troops in Konkrook into action. Keeluk doesn't have radio or TV—we hope—but he has his forces concentrated, and he has a pretty good staff."

"But Mr. Keeluk's a friend of ours. He knows what our Association is trying to do for his people...."

"So he shows his appreciation by setting that mob on you. Look, he has a lot of influence in that section. When you were attacked, why wasn't he out trying to quiet the mob?"

"When they jumped you, you tried to get back into the house," M'zangwe put in. "And you found the door barred against you."

"Yes, but...." The girl looked troubled; M'zangwe had guessed right. "But what's all the excitement about the dog? What is it, the sacred totem-animal of the Ullr Company?"

"It's just a big brown collie named Stalin. But somebody stole it, and Keeluk was keeping it. We want to know why. We don't like geek mysteries—not when they lead to murderous attacks on Terrans, at least."

It seemed to satisfy her, as the aircar let down on the hospital landing stage. But it didn't satisfy von Schlichten. He could smell trouble brewing. Just what could the geeks do with a dog? Nothing, so far as he could tell—but they didn't go in for such behaviour without what they considered good reason. Good for them, that is!

III

Governor-General Sidney Harrington had a ruddy outdoors-man's face and a ragged gray mustache; in his old tweed coat spotted with pipe ashes, he might have been any of a dozen-odd country-gentlemen of von Schlichten's boyhood in the Argentine. His face was composed enough for the part, too. But beyond him in the governor's office, Lieutenant-Governor Eric Blount matched von Schlichten's frown, his sandy-haired and younger face puckered in worry.

"We picked up a few of Keeluk's goon-gang," von Schlichten was reporting. "But I doubt if they'll tell us anything we don't already know. The dog was gone, but we found where it had been kept; at least one of the rabbits had been there, too. No trace of the goat. Anyhow, the riot's been put down. The Kragans and some of King Jaikark's infantry are patrolling the section. Jaikark's troops are busy making mass arrests. Either more slaves for the King's court favorites or else our Prime Minister Gurgurk wants to use them for patronage."

Blount nodded. "Gurgurk's building quite a political organization, lately. He must be about ready to shove Jaikark off the throne."

"Oh, Gurgurk wouldn't dare try anything like that," Harrington said. "He knows we wouldn't let him get away with it."

"Then why's he subsidizing this Mad Prophet Rakkeed?" Blount wanted to know. "Rakkeed is preaching a holy war against all Terrans and against Jaikark. Gurgurk subsidizes Rakkeed, and...."

"You haven't any proof of that," the governor protested.

Blount shrugged, his face looking grim. Von Schlichten knew how he felt. They couldn't prove it, but both knew that Rakkeed had been getting funds from the hands of Gurgurk. The prophet had been stepping up his crusade against the Terrans, and Gurgurk wasn't the only one backing him. The Prime Minister probably figured on using Rakkeed to stir up an outbreak; then Gurgurk could step in, after Jaikark was killed, put down the revolt he helped incite, and claim to be the best friend of the Company. But the question was whether Rakkeed could be used that way. He was becoming more of a menace than Gurgurk could ever be. Everywhere they turned, Rakkeed was at the bottom of their trouble—just in this case, where Keeluk was one of Rakkeed's followers.

His power seemed to be growing, too. There were rumors that he had been entertained at the palace in Keegark, just as he was usually entertained by the big shipowning nobles here at Konkrook; come to think of it, the last time here, he'd been guest of the Keegarkan ambassador. He went all over Ullr, crusading, traveling coolie-class in disguise on Company ships, according to their best information.

Blount sighed heavily. "This damned dog business worries me."

"Worries me, too," Harrington said. "I'm fond of that mutt, and God only knows what sort of stuff he's been getting to eat."

"I'm a lot more worried about why Keeluk was hiding him, and why he was willing to murder the only two Terrans on Konkrook who trust him, to prevent our finding out he had Stalin," Blount struck in.

Von Schlichten chain-lit another cigarette and stubbed out the old one. "Maybe Keeluk turned him over to Rakkeed to kill before a congregation of his followers—killing us in effigy. Or maybe they figure we worship Stalin, and getting him would give them power over us. I wish I knew a little more about Ullran psychology."

"One thing," Blount said. "It doesn't take any Ullran psychologist to know about eighty per cent of them hate us poisonously."

"Oh, rubbish!" Harrington blew the exclamation out around his pipe stem with a gush of smoke. "A few fanatics hate us, but nine-tenths of them have benefitted enormously from us."

"And hate us more deeply with each new benefit," Blount added. "They resent everything we've done for them."

"Yes, this spaceport proposition of King Orgzild of Keegark looks like it, doesn't it?" Harrington retorted. "He hates us so much he's offered us a spaceport at his city...."

"At what cost?" Blount asked. "He takes the land from some noble he executes for treason and gives it to us—together with forced labor. We furnish everything else. We get a port we don't need, and he gets all the business it'll bring. In fact, considering that Rakkeed is a welcome guest there, I wonder if he isn't fomenting trouble here at Konkrook to make us move our main base to Keegark. He's so sure we'll accept already that he's started building two new power-reactors to handle the additional demand from increased business."

"Where's he getting the plutonium?" von Schlichten asked, suspiciously.

"He just bought four tons of it from us, off the *City of Pretoria*," Harrington replied.

"A hell of a lot of plutonium," Blount said. "I wonder if he has any idea of what else plutonium can be used for?"

"Oh, God, I hope not!" Harrington exclaimed. "Bosh! What about those letters Keeluk gave the Quinton girl?"

"All addressed to rabidly anti-Terran Rakkeed disciples," von Schlichten replied. "We couldn't find any indication of a cipher, but the gossip about Keeluk's friends might have had code-meanings. I'll have to advise her to have nothing to do with any of the people Keeluk gave her letters to."

"Think she'll listen to you? These Extraterrestrial Rights Association people are a lot of blasted fanatics, themselves. They think we're a gang of bloody-fisted, flint-hearted imperialists."

"Oh, they're not as bad as all that. Old Mohammed Ferriera's always been decent enough. And the Association's really done a lot of good in other places."

A calculating look came into Harrington's eye. "She was going to Skilk, eh? And you're going there yourself, to investigate some of this Rakkeed worry of Eric's. Why not invite her along, and maybe you can plant a couple of ideas where they'll do the most good. We all know there are a lot of things at the polar mines that would look bad to anybody who didn't understand. And with all this trouble being stirred up now...."

It was his first admission that there *was* trouble, but von Schlichten let it pass. "Her company wouldn't be any heavy cross to bear," he replied. "I won't guarantee anything, of course...."

The intercom-speaker on the table whistled, and Harrington flipped a switch and spoke into the box. "Governor," a voice replied out of it, "there's a geek procession just landed from a water-barge in front, coming up the roadway to Company House. A platoon of Jaikark's Household Guards with a royal litter, Spear of State, gift-litter, nobles and such."

"Gurgurk with indemnity for the riot, eh? Let them in, give them an honor guard of Kragans, but keep their own gun-toters outside. Take them to Reception Hall until I signal from Audience Hall, then herd them in." He flipped back the switch and turned back. "We'll have to let them wait or they'll think we're worried. But you see—everything's going along normal lines."

Blount nodded, but his face showed disbelief. And von Schlichten grumbled unhappily to himself, without knowing why, until they finally went out to the big Audience Hall to meet the delegation.

Governor-General Sidney Harrington, on the comfortably-upholstered bench on the dais of the Audience Hall, didn't look particularly regal. But then, to a Terran, any of the kings of Ullr would have looked like a freak birth in a lizard-house at a zoo; it was hard to guess what impression Harrington would make on the Ullran psychology.

He took the false palate and tongue-clicker, officially designated as an "enunciator, Ullran" and, colloquially, as a geek-speaker, out of his coat pocket and shoved it into his mouth. Von Schlichten and Blount put in theirs, and Harrington pressed the floor-button with his toe. After a brief interval, the wide doors at the other end of the hall slid open, and the Konkrookan notables, attended by a dozen Company native-officers and a guard of Kragan Rifles, entered. The honor-guard advanced in two columns; between them marched an unclad and heavily armed native carrying an ornate spear with a three-foot blade upright in front of him with all four hands. It was the Konkrookan Spear of State; it represented the proxy-presence of King Jaikark. Behind it stalked Gurgurk, the Konkrookan equivalent of Prime Minister or Grand Vizier; he wore a gold helmet and a thing like a string-vest made of gold wire, and carried a long sword with a two-hand grip, a pair of Terran automatics built for a hand with six-four-knuckled fingers, and a pair of matched daggers. He was considerably past the Ullran prime of life—seventy or eighty, to judge from the worn appearance of his opal teeth, the color of his skin, and the predominantly reddish tint of his quartz-speckles. The retinue of nobles behind Gurgurk ran through the whole spectrum, from a princeling who was almost oyster-gray to the Keegarkan Ambassador, who was even blacker and more red-speckled than Gurgurk.

Four slaves brought up in the rear, carrying an ornately inlaid box on poles. When the spear-bearer reached the exact middle of the hall, he halted and grounded his regalia-weapon with a thump. Gurgurk came up and halted a couple of paces behind and to the left of the spear, and most of the other nobles drew up in two curved lines some ten paces to the rear; the ambassador and another noble came up and planted themselves beside Gurgurk.

*

The Governor-General rose slowly and descended from the dais, advancing to within ten paces of the Spear, von Schlichten and Blount accompanying him.

"Welcome, Gurgurk," Harrington gibbered through his false palate. "The Company is honored by this visit."

"I come in the name of my royal master, His Sublime and Ineffable Majesty, Jaikark the Seventeenth, King of Konkrook and of all the lands of the Konk Isthmus," Gurgurk squeaked and clicked. "I have the honor to bring with me the Lord Ambassador of King Orgzild of Keegark to the court of my royal master."

"And I," the ambassador said, after being suitably welcomed, "am honored to be accompanied by Prince Gorkrink, special envoy from my master, His Royal and Imperial Majesty King Orgzild, who is in your city to receive the shipment of power-metal my royal master has been honored to be permitted to purchase from the Company."

More protocol about welcoming Gorkrink. Then Gurgurk cleared his throat with a series of barking sounds.

"My royal master, His Sublime and Ineffable Majesty, is prostrated with grief," he stated solemnly. "Were his sorrow not so overwhelming, he would have come in His Own Sacred Person to express the pain and shame which he feels that people of the Company should be set upon and endangered in the streets of the royal city."

"The soldiers of His Sublime and Ineffable Majesty came most promptly to the aid of the troops of the Company, did they not, General von Schlichten?" Harrington asked, solemn-faced.

"Within minutes, Your Excellency," von Schlichten replied gravely. "Their promptness, valor and efficiency were most exemplary."

*

Gurgurk spoke at length, expressing himself as delighted, on behalf of his royal master, at hearing such high praise from so distinguished a soldier. Eric Blount contributed a short speech, beseeching the gods that the deep and beautiful friendship existing between the Chartered Ullr Company and His Sublime etcetera would continue unimpaired. The Keegarkan Ambassador spoke his piece, expressing on behalf of King Orgzild the deepest regret that the people of the Company should be so molested, and managing to hint that things like that simply didn't happen at Keegark.

The Prince Gorkrink then spoke briefly, in sympathy. Von Schlichten noticed that a few of his more recent quartz-specks were slightly greenish in tinge, a sure sign that he had, not long ago, been exposed to the fluorine-tainted air which men and geeks alike breathed on Niflheim. When a geek prince hired out as a laborer for a year on Niflheim, he did so for only one purpose—to learn Terran technologies.

Gurgurk then announced that so enormous a crime against the friends of His Sublime etcetera had not been allowed to go unpunished, signalling behind him with one of his lower hands for the box to be brought forward. The slaves carried it to the front, set it down, and opened it, taking from it a rug which they spread on the floor. On this, from the box, they placed twenty-four newly severed opal-grinning heads, in four neat rows. They had all been freshly scrubbed and polished, but they still smelled like crushed cockroaches.

The three Terrans looked at them gravely. A double-dozen heads was standard payment for an attack in which no Terran had been killed. Ostensibly, they were the heads of the ringleaders; in practice, they were usually lopped from the first two-dozen prisoners or overage slaves at hand, without regard for whether the victims had ever heard of the crime they were expiating.

There was another long speech from Gurgurk, with the nobles behind him murmuring antiphonal agreement—standard procedure, for which there was a standard pun, geek chorus—and a speech of response from Sid Harrington. Standing stiffly through the whole rigamarole, von Schlichten waited for it to end, as, finally, it did.

They walked back from the door, whence they had escorted the delegation, and stood looking down at the saurian heads on the rug. Harrington raised his voice and called to a Kragan sergeant whose chevrons were painted on all four arms.

"Take this carrion out and stuff it in the incinerator," he ordered.

*

"Wait a minute," von Schlichten told the sergeant. Then he disgorged and pouched his geek-speaker. "See that head, there?" he asked, rolling it over with his toe. "I killed that geek, myself, with my pistol. And Hid O'Leary stuck a knife in that one." He walked around the rug, turning heads over with his foot. "This was a cut-rate head-payment; they just slashed off two-dozen heads at the scene of the riot. Six months ago, Gurgurk wouldn't have tried to pull anything like this. Now he's laughing up his non-existent sleeve at us."

"That's what I've been preaching, all along," Eric Blount took up after him. "These geeks need having the fear of Terra thrown into them."

"Oh, nonsense, Eric; you're just as bad as Carlos, here!" Harrington tut-tuted. "Next, you'll be saying that we ought to depose Jaikark and take control ourselves."

"Well, what's wrong with that, for an idea?" von Schlichten demanded.

"My God!" Harrington exploded. "Don't let me hear that kind of talk again! We're not *conquistadores*: we're employees of a business concern, here to make money honestly, by exchanging goods and services with these people...."

*

He turned and walked away, out of the Audience Hall, leaving von Schlichten and Blount to watch the removal of the geek-heads.

"You know, I went a little too far," von Schlichten confessed. "Or too fast, rather."

"We can't go too slowly, though," Blount replied.

Von Schlichten nodded seriously. "Did you notice the green specks in the hide of that Prince Gorkrink?" he asked. "He's just come back from Niflheim. Probably on the *Canberra*, three months ago."

"And he's here to get that plutonium, and ship it to Keegark on the *Oom Paul Kruger*," Blount considered. "I wonder just what he learned, on Niflheim."

"I wonder just what's going on at Keegark," von Schlichten said. "Orgzild's pulled down a regular First-Century-model iron curtain. You know, four of our best native Intelligence operatives have been murdered in Keegark in the last three months, and six more have just vanished there."

"Well, I'm going there in a few days, myself, to talk to Orgzild about this spaceport deal," Blount said. "I'll have a talk with Hendrik Lemoyne and Colonel MacKinnon. And I'll see what I can find out for myself."

"Well, let's go have a drink," von Schlichten suggested.

But he kept remembering the falsehood of Gurgurk's indemnity. When the Ullrans started making a mockery of such things, it was no time for Harrington's trusting policies. The smell of trouble was suddenly stronger in his nostrils.

ULLR UPRISING

IV

Von Schlichten and Blount entered the bar together. Going to a bartending machine, von Schlichten dialed the cocktail they had decided upon and inserted his key to charge the drinks to his account, filling a four-portion jug.

As they turned away, they almost collided with Hideyoshi O'Leary and Paula Quinton. The girl wore a long-sleeved gown to conceal a bandage on her right wrist, and her face was rather heavily powdered in spots; otherwise she looked none the worse for recent experiences. Von Schlichten invited her and her escort to join him and Blount. Colonel O'Leary was carrying a cocktail jug and a couple of glasses; finding a table out of the worst of the noise, they all sat down together.

"I suppose you think it's a joke, our being nearly murdered by the people we came to help," Paula began, a trifle defensively.

"Not a very funny joke," von Schlichten told her. "It's been played on us till it's lost its humor."

"Yes, geek ingratitude's an old story to all of us," Blount agreed. "You stay on this planet very long and you'll see what I mean."

"You call them that, too?" she asked, as though disappointed in him. "Maybe if you stopped calling them geeks, they wouldn't resent you the way they do. You know, that's a nasty name; in the First Century Pre-Atomic, it designated a degraded person who performed some sort of revolting public exhibition...."

"As far as that goes, you know what the geek name for a Terran is?" Blount asked. "*Suddabit.*"

She looked puzzled for a moment, then slipped in her enunciator. Even in the absence of any native, she used her handkerchief to mask the act.

"Suddabit," she said, distinctly. "Sud-da-a-*bit.*" Taking out the geek-speaker, she put it away. "Why, that's exactly how they'd pronounce it!"

"And don't tell me you haven't heard it before," O'Leary said. "The geeks were screaming it at you, over on Seventy-second Street, this afternoon. *Znidd suddabit*; kill the Terrans. That's Rakkeed the Prophet's whole gospel."

"So you see," Eric Blount rammed home the moral, "this is just another case of nobody with any right to call anybody else's kettle black.... Cigarette?"

24

*

"Thank you." She leaned toward the lighter-flame O'Leary had snapped into being. "I suspect that of being a principle you'd like me to bear in mind at the Polar mines, when I see, let's say, some laborer being beaten by a couple of overseers with three foot lengths of three-quarter-inch steel cable."

"If you think the natives who work at the mines feel themselves ill-treated, you might propose closing them down entirely and see what the native reaction would be," von Schlichten told her. "Independently-hired free workers can make themselves rich, by native standards, in a couple of seasons; many of the serfs pick up enough money from us in incentive-pay to buy their freedom after one season."

"Well, if the Company's doing so much good on this planet, how is it that this native, Rakkeed, the one you call the Mad Prophet, is able to find such a following?" Paula demanded. "There must be something wrong somewhere."

"That's a fair question," Blount replied, inverting a cocktail jug over his glass to extract the last few drops. "When we came to Ullr, we found a culture roughly like that of Europe during the Seventh Century Pre-Atomic. We initiated a technological and economic revolution here, and such revolutions have their casualties, too. A number of classes and groups got squeezed pretty badly, like the horse-breeders and harness-manufacturers on Terra by the invention of the automobile, or the coal and hydroelectric interests when direct conversion of nuclear energy to electric current was developed, or the railroads and steamship lines at the time of the discovery of the contragravity-field. Naturally, there's a lot of ill-feeling on the part of merchants and artisans who weren't able or willing to adapt themselves to changing conditions; they're all backing Rakkeed and yelling '*Znidd suddabit!*' now. But it is a fact, which not even Rakkeed can successfully deny, that we've raised the general living standard of this planet by about two hundred per cent."

*

Both jugs were empty. Colonel O'Leary, as befitted his junior rank, picked them up; after a good-natured wrangled with von Schlichten, Blount handed the colonel his credit-key.

"The merchants in the North don't like us; beside spoiling the caravan-trade, we're spoiling their local business, because the landowning barons, who used to deal with them, are now dealing directly with us. At Skilk, King Firkked's afraid his feudal nobility is going to force a Runnymede on him, so he's been currying favor with the urban merchants; that makes him as pro-Rakkeed and as anti-Terran as they are. At Krink, King Jonkvank has the support of his barons, but he's afraid of his urban bourgeoisie, and we pay him a handsome subsidy, so he's pro-Terran and anti-Rakkeed. At Skilk, Rakkeed comes and goes openly; at Krink he has a price on his head."

"Jonkvank is not one of the assets we boast about too loudly," Hideyoshi O'Leary said, pausing on his way from the table. "He's as bloody-minded an old murderer as you'd care not to meet in a dark alley."

"We can turn our backs on him and not expect a knife between our shoulders, anyhow," von Schlichten said. "And we can believe, oh, up to eighty per cent of what he tells us, and that's sixty per cent better than any of the other native princes, except King Kankad, of course. The Kragans are the only real friends we have on this planet." He thought for a moment. "Miss Quinton, are you doing sociographic research-work here, in addition to your Ex-Rights work?" he asked. "Well, let me advise you to pay some attention to the Kragans."

"Oh, but they're just a parasite-race on the Terrans," Dr. Paula Quinton objected. "You find races like that all through the explored Galaxy—pathetic cultural mongrels."

Both men laughed heartily. Colonel O'Leary, returning with the jugs, wanted to know what he'd missed. Blount told him.

"Ha! She's been reading that thing of Stanley-Browne's," he said.

"What's the matter with Stanley-Browne?" Paula demanded.

"Stanley-Browne is one author you can depend on," O'Leary assured her. "If you read it in Stanley-Browne, it's wrong. You know, I don't think she's run into many Kragans. We ought to take her over and introduce her to King Kankad."

*

Von Schlichten allowed himself to be smitten by an idea. "By Allah, so we had!" he exclaimed. "Look, you're going to Skilk, in the next week, aren't you? Well, do you think you could get all your end-jobs cleared up here and be ready to leave by 0800 Tuesday? That's four days from today."

"I'm sure I could. Why?"

"Well, I'm going to Skilk, myself, with the armed troopship *Aldebaran*. We're stopping at King Kankad's Town to pick up a battalion of Kragan Rifles for duty at the Polar mines, where you're going. Suppose we leave here in my command-car, go to Kankad's Town, and wait there till the *Aldebaran* gets in. That would give us about two to three hours. If you think the Kragans are 'pathetic cultural mongrels', what you'll see there will open your eyes. And I might add that the nearest Stanley-Browne ever came to seeing Kankad's Town was from the air, once, at a distance of more than four miles."

"Well, general, I'll take you up," she said. "But I warn you; if this is some scheme to indoctrinate me with the Ullr Company's side of the case and blind me to unjust exploitation of the natives here, I don't propagandize very easily."

"Fair enough, as long as you don't let fear of being propagandized blind you to the good we're doing here, or impair your ability to observe and draw accurate conclusions. Just stay scientific about it and I'll be satisfied. Now, let's take time out for lubrication," he said, filling her glass and passing the jug.

Two hours and five cocktails later, they were still at the table, and they had taught Paula Quinton some twenty verses of *The Heathen Geeks, They Wear No Breeks*, including the four printable ones.

*

Four days later they stood together as the aircar passed over the Kraggork Swamps—pleasantly close together, von Schlichten realized. For the moment, he could almost forget the queer, intangible tension that had been growing steadily, and the feeling that things were nearing a breaking point of some kind.

Von Schlichten was scanning the horizon ahead. He pulled over a pair of fifty-power binoculars on a swinging arm and put them where she could use them.

"Right ahead, there; just a little to the left. See that brown-gray spot on the landward edge of the swamp? That's King Kankad's Town. It's been there for thousands of years, and it's always been Kankad's Town. You might say, even the same Kankad. The Kragan kings have always provided their own heirs, by self-fertilization. The offspring is an exact duplicate of the single parent. The present Kankad speaks of his heir as 'Little Me,' which is a fairly accurate way of putting it."

He knew what she was seeing through the glasses—a massive butte of flint, jutting out into the swamp on the end of a sharp ridge, with a city on top of it. All the buildings were multi-storied, some piling upward from the top and some clinging to the sides. The high watchtower at the front now carried a telecast-director, aimed at an automatic relay-station on an unmanned orbiter two thousand miles off-planet.

"They're either swamp-people who moved up onto that rock, or they're mountaineers who came out that far along the ridges and stopped," she said. "Which?"

"Nobody's ever tried to find out. Maybe if you stay on Ullr long enough, you can. That ought to be good for about eight to ten honorary doctorates. And maybe a hundred sols a year in book royalties."

"Maybe I'll just do that, general.... What's that, on the little island over there?" she asked, shifting the glasses. "A clump of flat-roofed buildings. Under a red-and-yellow danger-flag."

"That's Dynamite Island; the Kragans have an explosives-plant there. They make nitroglycerine, like all the thalassic peoples; they also make TNT and propellants. Learned that from us, of course. They also manufacture most of their own firearms, some of them pretty extreme—up to 25-mm. for shoulder rifles. Don't ever fire one; it'd break every bone in your body."

"Are they that much stronger than us?"

He shook his head. "Just denser; heavier. They're about equal to us in weight-lifting. They can't run, or jump, as well as we can. We often come out here for games with the Kragans, where the geeks can't watch us. And that reminds me—you're right about that being a term of derogation, because I don't believe I've ever knowingly spoken of a Kragan as a geek, and in fact they've picked up the word from us and apply it to all non-Kragans. But as I was saying, our baseball team has to give theirs a handicap, but their football team can beat the daylights out of ours. In a tug-of-war, we have to put two men on our end for every one of theirs. But they don't even try to play tennis with us."

"Don't the other natives make their own firearms?"

"No, and we're not going to teach them how!"

H. BEAM PIPER

*

The aircar came in, circling slowly over the town on the big rock, and let down on the roof of the castle-like building from which the watchtower rose. There were a dozen or so individuals waiting for them—the five Terrans, three men and two women, from the telecast station, and the rest Kragans. One of these, dark-skinned but with speckles no darker than light amber, armed only with a heavy dagger, came over and clapped von Schlichten on the shoulder, grinning opalescently.

"Greetings, Von!" he squawked in Kragan, then, seeing Paula, switched over to the customary language of the Takkad Sea country. "It makes happiness to see you. How long will you stay with us?"

"Till the *Aldebaran* gets in from Konkrook, to pick up the Rifles," von Schlichten replied, in Lingua Terra. He looked at his watch. "Two hours and a half.... Kankad, this is Paula Quinton; Paula, King Kankad."

He took out his geek-speaker and crammed it into his mouth. Before any other race on Ullr, that would have been the most shocking sort of bad manners, without the token-concealment of the handkerchief. Kankad took it as a matter of course. At some length, von Schlichten explained the nature of Paula's sociographic work, her connection with the Extraterrestrials' Rights Association, and her intention of going to the Arctic mines. Kankad nodded.

"You were right," he said. "I wouldn't have understood all that in your language. If I had read it, maybe, but not if I heard it." He put his upper right hand on Paula's shoulder and uttered a clicking approximation of her name. He turned and introduced another Kragan, about his own age, who wore the equipment and insignia of a Company native-major and was freshly painted with the Company emblem. "This is Kormork. He and I have borne young to each other. Kormork, you watch over Paula Quinton." He managed, on the second try, to make it more or less recognizable. "Bring her back safe. Or else find yourself a good place to hide."

Kankad introduced the rest of his people, and von Schlichten introduced the Terrans from the telecast-station. Then Kankad looked at the watch he was wearing on his lower left wrist.

"We will have plenty of time, before the ship comes, to show Paula the town," he suggested. "Von, you know better than I do what she would like

29

to see."

*

He led the way past a pair of long 90-mm. guns to a stone stairway. Von Schlichten explained, as they went down, that the guns of King Kankad's town were the only artillery above 75-mm. on Ullr in non-Terran hands. They climbed into an open machine-gun carrier and strapped themselves to their seats, and for two hours King Kankad showed her the sights of the town. They visited the school, where young Kragans were being taught to read Lingua Terra and studied from textbooks printed in Johannesburg and Sydney and Buenos Aires. Kankad showed her the repair-shops, where two-score descendants of Kragan river-chieftains were working on contragravity equipment, under the supervision of a Scottish-Afrikaner and his Malay-Portuguese wife; the small-arms factory, where very respectable copies of Terran rifles and pistols and auto-weapons were being turned out; the machine-shop; the physics and chemistry labs; the hospital; the ammunition-loading plant; the battery of 155-mm. Long Toms, built in Kankad's own shops, which covered the road up the sloping rock-spine behind the city; the printing-shop and book-bindery; the observatory, with a big telescope and an ingenious orrery of the Beta Hydrae system; the nuclear-power plant, part of the original price for giving up brigandage.

Half an hour before the ship from Konkrook was due, they had arrived at the airport, where a gang of Kragans were clearing a berth for the *Aldebaran.* From somewhere, Kankad produced two cold bottles of Cape Town beer for Paula and von Schlichten, and a bowl of some boiling-hot black liquid for himself. Von Schlichten and Paula lit cigarettes; between sips of his bubbling hell brew, Kankad gnawed on the stalk of some swamp-plant. Paula seemed as much surprised at Kankad's disregard for the eating taboo as she had been at von Schlichten's open flouting of the convention of concealment when he had put in his geek-speaker.

"This is the only place on Ullr where this happens," von Schlichten told her. "Here, or in the field when Terran and Kragan soldiers are together. There aren't any taboos between us and the Kragans."

"No," Kankad said. "We cannot eat each others' food, and because our bodies are different, we cannot be the fathers of each others' young. But we have been battle-comrades, and work-sharers, and we have learned from each other, my people more from yours than yours from mine. Before you came, my people were like children, shooting arrows at little animals on the beach, and climbing among the rocks at dare-me-and-I-do, and playing war with toy weapons. But we are growing up, and it will not be long before we will stand beside you, as the grown son stands beside his parent, and when that day comes, you will not be ashamed of us."

*

It was easy to forget that Kankad had four arms and a rubbery, quartz-speckled skin, and a face like a lizard's.

"I want Little Me, when he's old enough to travel, to visit your world," Kankad said. "And some of the other young ones. And when Little Me is old enough to take over the rule of our people, I would like to go to Terra, myself."

"You're going," von Schlichten assured him. "Some day, when I return, I'll see that you make the trip with me."

"Wonderful, Von!" Kankad was silent for a moment. When he spoke again, it was in Kragan, and quickly. "If we live so long, old friend. There is trouble coming, though even my spies cannot find what that trouble is. And two days ago in Keegark, two of my people died trying to learn it. I ask you—be careful!"

Then he switched hastily back to the language Paula could understand, apologizing. It gave von Schlichten time to wipe the worry from his face before she turned back to him, though it was worse news than he had expected. If Kankad thought things were bad enough to add his own spies to those of the Company, things couldn't be much worse. In fact, anything that brought whatever it was out into the open would be better.

He was still fretting over it as they said their good-byes to Kankad and boarded the *Aldebaran* for Skilk.

V

The last clatter of silverware and dishes ceased as the native servants finished clearing the table. There was a remaining clatter of cups and saucers; liqueur-glasses tinkled, and an occasional cigarette-lighter clicked. At the head table, the voices seemed louder.

"... don't like it a millisol's worth," Brigadier-General Barney Mordkovitz, the Skilk military CO, was saying to the lady on his right. "They're too confounded meek. Nowadays, nobody yells '*Znidd suddabit!*'

31

at you. They just stand and look at you like a farmer looking at a turkey the week before Christmas, and that I don't like!"

"Oh, bosh!" Jules Keaveney, the Skilk Resident-Agent, at the head of the table, exclaimed. "If they don't bow and scrape to you and get off the sidewalk to let you pass, you say they're insolent and need a lesson. If they do, you say they're plotting insurrection."

"What I said," Mordkovitz repeated, "was that I expect a certain amount of disorder, and a certain minimum show of hostility toward us from some of these geeks, to conform to what I know to be our unpopularity with many of them. When I don't find it, I want to know why."

"I'm inclined," von Schlichten came to his subordinate's support, "to agree. This sudden absence of overt hostility is disquieting. Colonel Cheng-Li," he called on the local Intelligence officer and Constabulary chief. "This fellow Rakkeed was here, about a month ago. Was there any noticeable disorder at that time? Anti-Terran demonstrations, attacks on Company property or personnel, shooting at aircars, that sort of thing?"

"No more than usual, general. In fact, it was when Rakkeed came here that the condition General Mordkovitz was speaking of began to become conspicuous."

Von Schlichten nodded. "And I might say that Lieutenant-Governor Blount has reported from Keegark, where he is now, that the same unnatural absence of hostility exists there."

"Well, of course, general," Keaveney said patronizingly, "King Orgzild has things under pretty tight control at Keegark. He'd not allow a few fanatics to do anything to prejudice these spaceport negotiations."

*

"I wonder if the idea back of that spaceport proposition isn't to get us concentrated at Keegark, where Orgzild could wipe us all out in one surprise blow," somebody down the table suggested, and others nodded.

"Oh, Orgzild wouldn't be crazy enough to try anything like that," Commander Dirk Prinsloo, of the *Aldebaran*, declared. "He'd get away with it for just twelve months—the time it would take to get the news to Terra and for a Federation Space Navy task-force to get here. And then, there'd be little bits of radioactive geek floating around this system as far out as the orbit of Beta Hydrae VII."

"That's quite true," von Schlichten agreed. "The point is, does Orgzild know it? I doubt if he even believes there is a Terra."

"Then where in Space does he think we come from?" Keaveney demanded.

"I believe he thinks Niflheim is our home world," von Schlichten replied. "Or, rather, the string of orbiters and artificial satellites around Niflheim. Where he thinks Niflheim is, I wouldn't even try to guess."

"Yes. After he'd wiped us out, he might even consider the idea of an invasion of Niflheim with captured contragravity ships," Hideyoshi O'Leary chuckled. "That would be a big laugh—if any of us were alive, then, to do any laughing."

"You don't really believe that, general?" Keaveney asked. His tone was still derisive, but under the derision was uncertainty. After all, von Schlichten had been on Ullr for fifteen years, to his two.

"Any question of geek psychology is wide open as far as I'm concerned; the longer I stay here, the less I understand it." Von Schlichten finished his brandy and got out cigarette-case and lighter. "I have an idea of the sort of garbled reports these spies of his who spend a year on Niflheim as laborers bring back."

*

"You know the line Rakkeed's been taking, of course," Colonel Cheng-Li put in. "He as much as says that Niflheim's our home, and that the farms where we raise food, here, and those evergreen plantings on Konk Isthmus and between here and Grank are the beginning of an attempt to drive all native life from this planet and make it over for ourselves."

"And that savage didn't think an idea like that up for himself; he got it from somebody like Orgzild," the black-bearded brigadier-general added. "You know, the main base off Niflheim is practically self-supporting, with hyproponic-gardens and animal-tissue culture vats. And it's enough bigger than one of the *City* ships to pass for a little world. Yes; somebody like Orgzild, or King Firkked, here, could easily pick up the idea that that's our home planet."

"The Company ought to let us stockpile nuclear weapons here, just to be on the safe side," another officer, farther down the table, said.

"Well, I'm not exactly in favor of that," von Schlichten replied. "It's the same principle as not allowing guards who have to go in among the convicts to carry firearms. If somebody like Orgzild got hold of a nuclear bomb, even a little old First-Century H-bomb, he could use it for a model and construct a hundred like it, with all the plutonium we've been handing out for power reactors. And there are too few of us, and we're concentrated in too few places, to last long if that happened. What this planet needs, though, is a visit by a fifty-odd-ship task-force of the Space Navy, just to show the geeks what we have back of us. After a show like that, there'd be a lot less *znidd suddabit* around here."

"General, I deplore that sort of talk," Keaveney said. "I hear too much of this mailed-fist-and-rattling-sabre stuff from some of the junior officers here, without your giving countenance and encouragement to it. We're here to earn dividends for the stockholders of the Ullr Company, and we can only do that by gaining the friendship, respect and confidence of the natives...."

*

"Mr. Keaveney," Paula Quinton spoke. "I doubt if even you would seriously accuse the Extraterrestrials Rights Association of favoring what you call a mailed fist and rattling sabre policy. We've done everything in our power to help these people, and if anybody should have their friendship, we should. Well, only five days ago, in Konkrook, Mr. Mohammed Ferriera and I were attacked by a mob, our native aircar driver was murdered, and if it hadn't been for General von Schlichten and his soldiers, we'd have lost our own lives. Mr. Ferriera is still hospitalized as a result of injuries he received. It seems that General von Schlichten and his Kragans aren't trying to get friendship and confidence; they're willing to settle for respect, in the only way they can get it—by hitting harder and quicker than the natives can."

Somebody down the table—one of the military, of course—said, "Hear, hear!" Von Schlichten came as close as a man wearing a monocle can to winking at Paula. Good girl, he thought; she's started playing on the Army team, and about time!

"Well, of course...." Keaveney began. Then he stopped, as a Terran sergeant came up to the table and bent over Barney Mordkovitz' shoulder, whispering urgently. The black-bearded brigadier rose immediately, taking his belt from the back of his chair and putting it on. Motioning the sergeant to accompany, he spoke briefly to Keaveney and then came around the table to where von Schlichten sat, the Resident-Agent accompanying him.

"Message just came in from Konkrook, general," he said softly. "Governor Harrington's dead."

It took von Schlichten all of a second to grasp what had been said. "Good God! When? How?"

"Here's all we know, sir," the sergeant said, giving him a radioprint slip. "Came in ten minutes ago."

It was an all-station priority telecast. Governor-General Harrington had died suddenly, in his room, at 2210; there were no details. He glanced at his watch; it was 2243. Konkrook and Skilk were in the same time-zone; that was fast work. He handed the slip to Mordkovitz, who gave it to Keaveney.

"You from the telecast station, sergeant?" he asked. "All right, in that case, let's go."

As he hurried from the banquet-room, he could hear Keaveney tapping on his wine-glass.

"Everybody, please! Let me have your attention! There has just come in a piece of the most tragic news...."

*

A woman captain met him just inside the door of the big soundproofed room of the telecast station, next to the Administration Building.

"We have a wavelength open to Konkrook, general," she said. "In booth three."

Another girl, a tech-sergeant, was in the booth; on the screen was the image of a third young woman, a lieutenant, at Konkrook station. The sergeant rose and started to leave the booth.

"Stick around, sergeant," von Schlichten told her. "I'll want you to take over when I'm through." He sat down in front of the combination visiscreen and pickup. "Now, lieutenant; just what happened?" he asked. "How did he die?"

"We think it was poison, general. General M'zangwe has ordered autopsy and chemical analysis. If you can wait about ten minutes, he'll be able to talk to you, himself."

"Call him. In the meantime, give me everything you know."

"Well, at about 2210, the Kragan guard-sergeant on that floor heard ten pistol-shots, as fast as they could be fired semi-auto, in the governor's

35

room. The door was locked, but he shot it off with his own pistol and went in. He found Governor Harrington on the floor, wearing only his gown, holding an empty pistol. He was in convulsions, frothing at the mouth, in horrible pain. Evidently he'd fired his pistol, which he kept on his desk, to call help; all the bullets had gone into the ceiling. One of the medics got there in five minutes, just as he was dying. He'd written his diary up to noon of today, and broken off in the middle of a word. There was a bottle and an overturned glass on his desk. The Constabulary got there a few minutes later, and then Brigadier-General M'zangwe took charge. A white rat, given fifteen drops from the whiskey-bottle, died with the same symptoms in about ninety seconds."

"Who had access to the whiskey-bottle?"

"A geek servant, who takes care of the room. He was caught, an hour earlier, trying to slip off the island without a pass; they were holding him at the guardhouse when Governor Harrington died. He's now being questioned by the Kragans." The girl's face was bleakly remorseless. "I hope they do plenty to him!"

"I hope they don't kill him before he talks."

*

"Wait a moment, general; we have General M'zangwe, now," the girl said. "I'll switch you over."

The screen broke into a kaleidoscopic jumble of color, then cleared; the chocolate-brown face of M'zangwe was looking out of it.

"I heard what happened, how they found him, and about that geek chamber-valet being arrested," von Schlichten said. "Did you get anything out of him?"

"He's admitted putting poison in the bottle, but he claims it was his own idea. But he's one of Father Keeluk's parishioners, so...."

"Keeluk! God damn, so that was it!" von Schlichten almost shouted. "Now I know what he wanted with Stalin, and that goat, and those rabbits! Of course they'd need terrestrial animals, to find out what would poison a Terran! Who's in charge at Konkrook now?"

"Not much of anybody. Laviola, the Fiscal Secretary, and Hans Meyerstein, the Banking Cartel's lawyer, and Howlett, the Personnel Chief, and Buhrmann, the Commercial Secretary, have made up a sort of quadrumvirate and are trying to run things. I don't know what would happen if anything came up suddenly...." A blue-gray uniformed arm, with a major's cuff-braid, came into the screen, handing a slip of paper to M'zangwe; he took it, glanced at it, and swore. Von Schlichten waited until he had read it through.

"Well, something has, all right," the African said. "Just got a call from Jaikark's palace—a revolt's broken out, presumably headed by Gurgurk; Household Guards either mutinied or wiped out by the mutineers, all but those twenty Kragan Rifles we loaned Jaikark. They, and about a dozen of Jaikark's courtiers and their personal retainers, are holding the approaches to the King's apartments. The native-lieutenant in charge of the Kragans just radioed in; says the situation is desperate."

"When a Kragan says that, he means damn near hopeless. Is this being recorded?" When M'zangwe nodded, he continued. "All right. Use the recording for your authority and take charge. I'm declaring martial rule at Konkrook, as of now, 2258. Tell Eric Blount what's happened, and what you've done, as soon as you can get in touch with him at Keegark. I'm leaving for Konkrook at once! I ought to get in by 0800.

"Now, as to the trouble at the Palace. Don't commit more than one company of Kragans and ten airjeeps and four combat-cars, and tell them to evacuate Jaikark and his followers and our Kragans to Gongonk Island. And alert your whole force. These geek palace revolutions are always synchronized with street-rioting, and this thing seems to have been synchronized with Sid Harrington's death, too. Get our Kragans out if you can't save anybody else from the Palace, but sacrificing thirty or forty men to save twenty is no kind of business. And keep sending reports; I can pick them up on my car radio as I come down." He turned to the girl Sergeant. "Keep on this; there'll be more coming in."

*

He rose and left the booth. If we can pull Jaikark's bacon off the fire, he was thinking, the Company can dictate its own terms to him afterward; if Jaikark's killed, we'll have Gurgurk's head off for it, and then take over Konkrook. In either case, it'll be a long step toward getting rid of all these geek despots. And with Eric Blount as Governor-General....

The inner door of the soundproofed telecast-room burst open, three men hurried inside, and it slammed shut behind them. In the brief interval, there had been firing audible from outside. One of the men had a pistol in his right hand, and with his left arm he supported a companion, whose shoulder was mangled and dripped blood. The third man had a burp-gun in his hands. All were in civilian dress—shorts and light jackets. The man with the pistol holstered it and helped his injured companion into a chair. The burp-gunner advanced into the room, looked around, saw von Schlichten, and addressed him.

"General! The geeks turned on us!" he cried. "The Tenth North Ullr's mutinied; they're running wild all over the place. They've taken their barracks and supply-buildings, and the lorry-hangars and the maintenance-yard; they're headed this way in a mob. Some of the Zirk Cavalry's joined them."

"Have any ammo left for that burp-gun? Come on, then; let's see what it's like at Company House," von Schlichten said. "Captain Malavez, you know what to do about defending this station. Get busy doing it. And have that girl in booth three tell Konkrook what's happened here, and say that I won't be coming down, as I planned, just yet."

He opened the door, and the rattle of shots outside became audible again. The civilian with the burp-gun knew better than to let a general go out first; elbowing von Schlichten out of the way, he crouched over his weapon and dashed outside. Drawing his pistol, von Schlichten followed, pulling the door shut after him.

*

Darkness had fallen, while he had been inside; now the whole Company Reservation was ablaze with electric lights. Somebody at the power-plant had thrown on the emergency lights. There was a confused mass of gray-skinned figures in front of Company House, reflected light twinkling on steel over them; from the direction of the native-troops barracks more natives were coming on the run. On the roof of a building across the street, two machine-guns were already firing into the mob. From up the street, a hundred-odd saurian-faced native soldiers were coming at the double, bayonets fixed and rifles at high port; with them ran several Terrans. Motioning his companion to follow, von Schlichten ran to meet them, falling in beside a Terran captain who ran in front.

"What's the score, captain?" he asked the panting captain.

"Tenth North Ullr and the Fifth Cavalry have mutinied; so have these rag-tag Auxiliaries. That mob down there's part of them." He was puffing under the double effort of running and talking. "Whole thing blew up in seconds; no chance to communicate with anybody...."

A Terran woman, in black slacks and an orange sweater, ran across the street in front of them, pursued by a group of enlisted "men" of the Tenth North Ullr Native Infantry, all shrieking "*Znidd suddabit!*" The fugitive ran into a doorway across the street; before her pursuers were aware of their danger, the Kragans had swept over them. There was no shooting; the slim, cruel-bladed bayonets did the work. From behind him, as he ran, von Schlichten could hear Kragan voices in a new cry: "*Znidd geek! Znidd geek!*"

The mob were swarming up onto the steps and into the semi-rotunda of the storm-porch. There was shooting, which told him that some of the humans who had been at the banquet were still alive. He wondered, half-sick, how many, and whether they could hold out till he could clear the doorway, and, most of all, he found himself thinking of Paula Quinton. Skidding to a stop within fifty yards of the mob, he flung out his arms crucifix-wise to halt the Kragans. Behind, he could hear the Terrans and native-officers shouting commands to form front.

"Give them one clip, reload, and then give them the bayonet!" he ordered. "Shove them off the steps and then clear the porch!"

The hundred rifles let go all at once; and for five seconds they poured a deafening two thousand rounds into the mutineers. There was some fire in reply; a Zirk corporal narrowly missed him with a pistol; he saw the captain's head fly apart when an explosive rifle-bullet hit him, and half a dozen Kragans went down.

"Reload! Set your safeties!" von Schlichten bellowed. "Charge!"

*

Under human officers, the North Ullr Native Infantry would have stood firm. Even under their native-officers and sergeants, they should not have broken as they did, but the best of these had paid for their loyalty to the Company with their lives. At that, the Skilkan peasantry who made up the Tenth Infantry, and the Zirk cavalrymen, tried briefly to fight as individuals, shrieking "*Znidd suddabit!*" until the Kragans were upon them, stabbing and shooting. They drove the rioters from the steps or killed them there, they wiped out those who had gotten into the semicircle of the storm-porch. The inside doors, von Schlichten saw, were open, but beyond them were Terrans and a dozen or so Kragans. Hideyoshi O'Leary and Barney Mordkovitz seemed to be in command of these.

"We had about thirty seconds' warning," Mordkovitz reported, "and the Kragans in the hall bought us another sixty seconds. Of course, we all had our pistols...."

"Hey! These storm-doors are wedged!" somebody discovered. "Those goddam geek servants ...!"

"Yeah; kill any of them you catch," somebody else advised. "If we could have gotten these doors closed...."

The mob, driven from the steps, was trying to re-form and renew the attack. From up the street, the machine-guns, silent during the bayonet-fight, began hammering again. The mob surged forward to get out of their fire, and were met by a rifle-blast and a hedge of bayonets at the steps; they surged back, and the machine-guns flailed them again. They started to rush the building from whence the automatic-fire came, and there was a fusilade and a shriek of "*Znidd geek!*" from up the street. They turned and fled in the direction from whence they had come, bullets scourging them from three directions at once.

For a moment, von Schlichten and the three Terrans and eighty-odd Kragans who had survived the fight stood on the steps, weapons poised, seeking more enemies. The machine-guns up the street stuttered a few short bursts and were silent. From behind, the beleaguered Terrans and their Kragan guards were emerging. He saw Jules Keaveney and his wife; Commander Prinsloo of the *Aldebaran*; Harry Quong and Bogdanoff. Ah, there she was! He heaved a breath of relief and waved to her.

The Kragans were already setting about their after-battle chores. A couple of hundred more Kragans, led by Native-Major Kormork, the co-parent of young with King Kankad, came up at the double and stopped in front of Company House.

*

"We were in quarters, aboard the *Aldebaran* and in the guest-house at the airport," Kormork reported. "We were attacked, fifteen minutes ago, by a mob. We took ten minutes beating them off, and five more getting here. I sent Native-Captain Zeerjeek and the rest of the force to re-take the supply-depot and the shops and lorry hangars, which had been taken, and relieve the military airport, which is under attack."

"Good enough. I hope you didn't spread yourself out too thin. What's the situation at the commercial airport?"

"The two ships, the *Aldebaran* and the freighter *Northern Star*, are both safe," Kormork replied. "I saw them go on contragravity and rise to about a hundred feet."

"Whose crowd is that you have?" he asked the Terran lieutenant who had taken over command of the first force of Kragans.

"Company 6, Eighteenth Rifles, sir. We were on duty at the guardhouse; fighting broke out in the direction of the native barracks. A couple of runners from Captain Retief of Company 4 came in with word that he was being attacked by mutineers from the Tenth N.U.N.I., but that he was holding them back. So Captain Charbonneau, who was killed a few minutes ago, left a Terran lieutenant and a Kragan native-lieutenant and a couple of native-sergeants and thirty Kragans to hold the guardhouse, and brought the rest of us here."

Von Schlichten nodded. "You'd pass the military airport and the power-plant, wouldn't you?" he asked.

"Yes, sir. The military airport's holding out, and I saw the red-and-yellow danger-lights on the fence around the power-plant."

That meant the power-plant was, for the time, safe; somebody'd turned twenty thousand volts into the fence.

"All right. I'm setting up my command post at the telecast station, where the communication equipment is." He turned to the crowd that had come out onto the porch from inside. "Where's Colonel Cheng-Li?"

"Here, general." The Intelligence and Constabulary officer pushed through the crowd. "I was on the phone, talking to the military airport, the commercial airport, ordnance depot, spaceport, ship-docks and power plant. All answer. I'm afraid Pop Goode, at the city power-plant, is done for; nobody answers there, but the TV-pickup is still on in the load-dispatcher's room, and the place is full of geeks. Colonel Jarman's coming here with a lorry to get combat-car crews; he's short-handed. Port-Captain Leavitt has all the native labor at the airport and spaceport herded into a repair dock; he's keeping them covered with the forward 90-mm. gun of the *Northern Star*. Lorry-hangars, repair-shops and maintenance-yards don't answer."

"That's what I was going to ask you. Good enough. Harry Quong,

Hassan Bogdanoff!"

His command-car crew front-and-centered.

"I want you to take Colonel O'Leary up, as soon as my car's brought here.... Hid, you go up and see what's going on. Drop flares where there isn't any light. And take a look at the native-labor camp and the equipment-park, south of the reservation.... Kormork, you take all your gang, and half these soldiers from the Eighteenth, here, and help clear the native-troops barracks. And don't bother taking any prisoners; we can't spare personnel to guard them."

Kormork grinned. The taking of prisoners had always been one of those irrational Terran customs which no Ullran regarded with favor, or even comprehension.

*

VI

There was fresh intelligence from Konkrook, by the time he returned to the telecast station. Mutiny had broken out there among the laborers and native troops, who outnumbered the Terrans and their Kragan mercenaries on Gongonk Island by five thousand to five hundred and fifteen hundred respectively. The attempt to relieve Jaikark's palace had been called off before the relief-force could be sent; there was heavy and confused fighting all over the island, and most of the combat contragravity and about half the Kragan Rifles had had to be committed to defend the Company farms across the Channel, on the mainland, south of the city. There had also been an urgent call for help from Colonel Rodolfo MacKinnon, in command of Company troops at the Keegark Residency.

He called Keegark; a girl, apparently one of the civilian telecast technicians, answered.

"We must have help, General von Schlichten," she told him. "The native troops, all but two hundred Kragans, have mutinied. They have everything here except Company House—docks, airport, everything. We're trying to hold out, but there are thousands of them."

"What happened to Eric Blount and your Resident-Agent, Mr. Lemoyne?"

"We don't know. They were at the Palace, talking to King Orgzild. We've tried to call the Palace, but we can't get through. General, we must have help...."

H. BEAM PIPER

A call came in, a few minutes later, from Krink, five hundred miles to the north-east across the mountains; the Resident-Agent there, one Francis Xavier Shapiro, reported rioting in the city and an attempted palace-revolution against King Jonkvank, and that the Residency was under attack. By way of variety, it was the army of King Jonkvank that had mutinied; the Sixth North Ullr Native Infantry and the two companies of Zirk cavalry at Krink were still loyal, along with the Kragans.

*

There was a pattern to all this. Von Schlichten stood staring at the big map, on the wall, showing the Takkad Sea area at the Equatorial Zone, and the country north of it to the Pole, the area of Ullr occupied by the Company. He was almost beginning to discern the underlying logic of the past half-hour's events when Keaveney, the Skilk Resident, blundered into him in a half-daze.

"Sorry, general; didn't see you." His face was ashen, and his jowls sagged. "My God, it's happening all over Ullr! Why, it's the end of all of us!"

"It's not quite that bad, Mr. Keaveney." He looked at his watch. It was now nearly an hour since the native troops here at Skilk had mutinied. Insurrections like this usually succeeded or failed in the first hour. "If we all do our part, we'll come out of it all right," he told Keaveney, more cheerfully than he felt, then turned to ask Brigadier-General Mordkovitz how the fighting was going at the native-troops barracks.

"Not badly, general. Colonel Jarman's got some contragravity up and working. They blew out all four of the Tenth N.U.N.I.'s barracks; the Tenth and the Zirks are trying to defend the cavalry barracks. Some of our Kragans managed to slip around behind the cavalry stables. They're leading out hipposaurs, and sniping at the rear of the cavalry barracks."

"That'll give us some cavalry of our own; a lot of these Kragans are good riders.... How about the repair-shops and maintenance-yard and lorry-hangars? I don't want these geeks getting hold of that equipment and using it against us."

"Kormork's outfit are trying to take back the lorry-hangars. Jarman's got a couple of airjeeps and a combat-car helping them."

"... won't be one of us left by this time tomorrow," Keaveney was wailing, to Paula Quinton and another woman. "And the Company is finished!"

Colonel Cheng-Li, the Intelligence officer, approached Keaveney and tried to quiet him. At the same time, a woman in black slacks and an orange sweater—the one whose pursuers had been overrun by the Kragans at the beginning of the fighting—approached von Schlichten.

"General; King Kankad's calling," she said. "He's on the screen in booth four."

*

Kankad's face was looking out of the screen at him, with Phil Yamazaki, the telecast operator at Kankad's Town, standing behind him.

"Von!" The Kragan spoke almost as though in physical pain. "What can I do to help? I have twenty thousand of my people here who are capable of bearing arms, all with firearms, but I have transport for only five hundred. Where shall I send them?"

Von Schlichten thought quickly. Keegark was finished; the Residency stood in the middle of the city, surrounded by two hundred thousand of King Orgzild's troops and subjects. Sending Kankad's five hundred warriors and his meager contragravity there would be the same as shovelling them into a furnace. The people at Keegark would have to be written off, like the twenty Kragans at Jaikark's palace.

"Send them to Konkrook," he decided. "Them M'zangwe's in command, there; he'll need help to hold the Company farms. Maybe he can find additional transport for you. I'll call him."

"I'll send off what force I can, at once," Kankad promised. "How does it go with you at Skilk?"

"We're holding, so far," he replied.

Captain Inez Malavez, the woman officer in charge of the station, put her head into the booth.

"General! Immediate-urgency message from Colonel O'Leary," she said. "Native laborers from the mine-labor camp are pouring into the mine-equipment park. Colonel O'Leary's used all his rockets and mg-ammunition trying to stop them."

"Call you back, later," von Schlichten told Kankad. "I'll see what Them M'zangwe can do about transport; get what force you can started for Konkrook at once."

He left the booth. "Barney!" he called. "General Mordkovitz! Who's the ranking officer in direct contact with the Eighteenth Rifles? Major

44

Falkenberg?"

"That's right."

"Well, tell him to get as many of his Kragans as he can spare down to the equipment-park." He turned to Inez Malavez. "You call Jarman; tell him what O'Leary reported, and tell him to get cracking on it. Tell him not to let those geeks get any of that equipment onto contragravity; knock it down as fast as they try to lift out with it. And tell him to see what he can do in the way of troop-carriers or lorries, to get Falkenberg's Rifles to the equipment-park.... How's business at the lorry-hangars and maintenance-yard?"

"Kormork's still working on that," the girl captain told him. "Nothing definite, yet."

*

In one corner of the big room, somebody had thumbtacked a ten-foot-square map of the Company area to the floor. Paula Quinton and Mrs. Jules Keaveney were on their knees beside it, pushing out handfuls of little pink and white pills that somebody had brought in two bottles from the dispensary across the road, each using a billiard-bridge. The girl in the orange sweater had a handful of scribbled notes, and was telling them where to push the pills. There were other objects on the map, too—pistol-cartridges, and cigarettes, and foil-wrapped food-concentrate wafers. Paula, seeing him, straightened.

"The pink are ours, general," she said. "The white are the geeks." Von Schlichten suppressed a grin; that was the second time he'd heard her use that word, this evening. "The cigarettes are airjeeps, the cartridges are combat-cars, and the wafers are lorries or troop-carriers."

"Not exactly regulation map-markers, but I've seen stranger things used.... Captain Malavez!"

"Yes, sir?" The girl captain, rushing past, her hands full of teleprint-sheets, stopped in mid-stride.

"What we need," he told her, "is a big TV-screen, and a pickup mounted on some sort of a contragravity vehicle at about two to five thousand feet directly overhead, to give us an image of the whole area. Can do?"

"Can try, sir. We have an eight-foot circular screen that ought to do all right for two thousand feet. I'll implement that at once."

Going into a temporarily idle telecast booth, he called Konkrook, and

45

finally got Themistocles M'zangwe on the screen.

"How is it, now?" he asked.

"Getting a little better," the Graeco-African replied. "Half an hour ago, we were shooting geeks out the windows, here; now we have them contained between the spaceport and the native-troops and labor barracks, and down the east side of the island to the farms. We have the wire around the farms on the island electrified, and we're using almost all our combat contragravity to keep the farms on the mainland clear." He hesitated for a moment. "Did you hear about Eric Blount and Lemoyne?"

Von Schlichten shook his head.

*

"The whole party that were at Orgzild's palace were massacred. Some of them were lucky enough to get killed fighting. The geeks took Eric and Hendrik alive; rolled them in a puddle of thermoconcentrate fuel and set fire to them. When we can spare the contragravity, we're going to drop something on the Kee-geek embassy, over in town."

Von Schlichten grimaced, but he'd expected something like it. He told M'zangwe about King Kankad's offer. "His crowd ought to be coming in in a couple of hours. What can you scrape up to send to Kankad's Town to airlift Kragans in?"

"Well, we have three hundred-and-fifty-foot gun-cutters, one 90-mm. apiece. The *Elmoran*, the *Gaucho*, and the *Bushranger*. But they're not much as transports, and we need them here pretty badly. Then, we have five fertilizer and charcoal scows, and a lot of heavy transport lorries, and two one-eighty-foot pickup boats."

"How about the *Piet Joubert?*" von Schlichten asked. "She was due in Konkrook from the east about 1300 today, wasn't she?"

M'zangwe swore. "She got in, all right. But the geeks boarded her at the dock, within twenty minutes after things started. They tried to lift out with her, and the Channel Battery shot her down into Konkrook Channel, off the Fifty-sixth Street docks."

"Well, you couldn't let the geeks have her, to use against us. What do you hear from the other ships?"

"*Procyon's* at Grank; we haven't had any reports of any kind from there, which doesn't look so good. The *Northern Lights* is at Grank, too. The *Oom Paid Kruger* should have been at Bwork, in the east, when the gun went off.

And the *Jan Smuts* and the *Christiaan De Wett* were both at Keegark; we can assume Orgzild has both of them."

"All right. I'm sending *Aldebaran* to Kankad's, to pick up more reenforcements for you."

*

Leaving the booth, he heard, above the clatter of communications-machines and the hubbub of voices, Jules Keaveney arguing contentiously. Evidently Colonel Cheng-Li's efforts to drag the Resident out of his despondency had been an excessive success.

"But it's crazy! Not just here; everywhere on Ullr!" Keaveney was saying. "How did they do it? They have no telecast equipment."

"You have me stopped, Jules," Mordkovitz was replying. "I know a lot of rich geeks have receiving sets, but no sending sets."

The pattern that had been tantalizing von Schlichten took visible shape in his mind. For a moment, he shelved the matter of the *Aldebaran*.

"They didn't need sending equipment, Barney," he said. "They used ours. Sid Harrington was poisoned in Konkrook. The news, of course, was sent out at once, as the geeks knew it would be, to every residency and trading-station on Ullr, and that was the signal they'd agreed upon, probably months in advance!"

"Well, what was our Intelligence doing; sleeping?" Keaveney demanded angrily.

"No; they were writing reports for your civil administration blokes to stuff in the wastebasket, and being called mailed-fist-and-rattling-sabre alarmists for their pains." He turned away from Keaveney. "Barney, where is Dirk Prinsloo?"

"Aboard his ship. He hitched a ride to the airport with Jarman, when he was here picking up air-crews."

"Call him. Tell him to take the *Aldebaran* to Kankad's Town, at once; as soon as he arrives there, which ought to be about 1100, he's to pick up all the Kragans he can pack aboard and take them to Konkrook. From then on, he'll be under Them M'zangwe's orders."

"To Konkrook?" Keaveney fairly howled. "Are you nuts? Don't you think we need reenforcements here, too?"

"Yes, I do. I'm going to try to get them," von Schlichten told him. "Now pipe down and get out of people's way."

47

He crossed the room, to where two Kragans, a male sergeant, and the ubiquitous girl in the orange sweater were struggling to get a big circular TV-screen up, then turned to look at the situation-map. A girl tech-sergeant was keeping Paula Quinton and Mrs. Jules Keaveney informed.

"Start pushing geeks out of the Fifth Zirk Cavalry barracks," the sergeant was saying. "The one at the north end, and the one next to it; they're both on fire, now." She tossed a slip into the wastebasket beside her and glanced at the next slip. "And more pink pills back of the barracks and stables, and move them a little to the north-west; Kragans as skirmishers, to intercept geeks trying to slip away from the cavalry barracks."

*

A young Kragan with his lower left arm in a sling and a daub of antiseptic plaster over the back of his head came up and gave him a radioprint slip. Guido Karamessinis, the Resident-Agent at Grank, had reported, at last. The city, he said, was quiet, but King Yoorkerk's troops had seized the Company airport and docks, taken the *Procyon* and the *Northern Lights* and put guards aboard them, and were surrounding the Residency. He wanted to know what to do.

Von Schlichten managed to get him on the screen, after awhile.

"It looks as though Yoorkerk's trying to play both sides at once," he told the Grank Resident. "If the rebellion's put down, he'll come forward as your friend and protector; if we're wiped out elsewhere, he'll yell '*Znidd suddabit!*' and swamp you. Don't antagonize him; we can't afford to fight this war on any more fronts than we are now. We'll try to do something to get you unfrozen, before long."

He called Krink again. A girl with red-gold hair and a dusting of freckles across her nose answered.

"How are you making out?" he asked.

"So far, fine, general. We're in complete control of the Company area, and all our native-troops, not just the Kragans, are with us. Jonkvank's pushed the mutineers out of his palace, and we're keeping open a couple of streets between there and here. We airlifted all our Kragans and half the Sixth N.U.N.I. to the Palace, and we have the Zirks patrolling the streets on 'saur-back. Now, we have our lorries and troop-carriers out picking up elements of Jonkvank's loyal troops outside town."

"Who's doing the rioting, then?"

48

She named three of Jonkvank's regiments. "And the city hoodlums, and priests from the temples of one sect that followed Rakkeed, and the whole passel of Skilkan fifth columnists."

"How long do you think it'd take, with the equipment you have, to airlift all of Jonkvank's loyal troops into the city?"

"Not before this time tomorrow."

"All right. Are you in radio communication with Jonkvank now?"

"Full telecast, audio-visual," the girl replied. "Just a minute, general."

*

He put in his geek-speaker. Within a few minutes, a saurian Ullran face was looking out of it at him; a harsh-lined, elderly, face, with an old scar, quartz-crusted, along one side.

"Your Majesty," von Schlichten greeted him.

Jonkvank pronounced something intended to correspond to von Schlichten's name. "We have image-met under sad circumstances, general," he said.

"Sad for both of us, King Jonkvank; we must help one another. I am told that your soldiers in Krink have risen against you, and that your loyal troops are far from the city."

"Yes. That was the work of my War Minister, Hurkkirk, who was in the pay of King Firkked of Skilk, may Jeels devour him alive! I have Hurkkirk's head here somewhere. I can have it found, if you want to see it."

"Dead-traitors' heads do not interest me, King Jonkvank," von Schlichten replied, in what he estimated that the Krinkan king would interpret as a tone of cold-blooded cruelty. "There are too many traitors' heads still on traitors' shoulders.... What regiments are loyal to you, and where are they now?"

Jonkvank began naming regiments and locating them, all at minor provincial towns at least a hundred miles from Krink.

"Hurkkirk did his work well; I'm afraid you killed him too mercifully," von Schlichten said. "Well, I'm sending the *Northern Star* to Krink. She can only bring in one regiment at a trip, the way they're scattered; which one do you want first?"

Jonkvank's mouth, until now compressed grimly, parted in a gleaming smile. He made an exclamation of pleasure which sounded rather like a boy running along a picket fence with a stick.

"Good, general! Good!" he cried. "The first should be the regiment Murderers, at Furnk; they all have rifles like your soldiers. Have them brought to the Great Square, at the Palace here. And then, the regiment Fear-Makers, at Jeelznidd, and the regiment Corpse-Reapers, at...."

"Let that go until the Murderers are in," von Schlichten advised. "They're at Furnk, you say? I'll send the *Northern Star* there, directly."

"Oh, good, general! I will not soon forget this! And, as soon as the work is finished here, I will send soldiers to help you at Skilk. There shall be a great pile of the heads of those who had part in this wickedness, both here and there!"

"Good. Now, if you will pardon me, I'll go to give the necessary orders...."

*

As he left the booth, he saw Hideyoshi O'Leary in front of the situation-map, and hailed him.

"Harry and Hassan are getting the car re-ammoed; they dropped me off here. Want to come up with us and see the show?" O'Leary asked, as he saw the general.

"No, I want you to go to Krink, as soon as Harry brings the car here again." He told O'Leary what he intended doing. "You'll probably have to go around ahead of the *Star* and alert these regiments. And as soon as things stabilize at Krink, prod Jonkvank into airlifting troops here. You're authorized, in my name, to promise Jonkvank that he can assume political control at Skilk, after we've stuffed Firkked's head in the dustbin."

Jules Keaveney, who always seemed to be where he wasn't wanted, heard that and fairly screamed.

"General von Schlichten! That is a political decision! You have no authority to make promises like that; that is a matter for the Governor-General, at least!"

"Well, as of now, and until a successor to Sid Harrington can be sent here from Terra, I'm Governor-General," von Schlichten told him, mentally thanking Keaveney for reminding him of the necessity for such a step. "Captain Malavez! You will send out an all-station telecast, immediately: Military Commander-in-Chief Carlos von Schlichten, being informed of the deaths of both Governor-General Harrington and Lieutenant-Governor Blount, assumes the duties of Governor-General, as of 0001 today." He turned to Keaveney. "Does that satisfy you?" he asked.

"No, it doesn't. You have no authority to assume a civil position of any sort, let alone the very highest position...."

Von Schlichten unbuttoned his holster and took out his authority, letting Keaveney look in to the muzzle of it.

"Here it is," he said. "If you're wise, don't make me appeal to it."

Keaveney shrugged. "I can't argue with that," he said. "But I don't fancy the Ullr Company is going to be impressed by it."

"The Ullr Company," von Schlichten replied, "is six and a half parsecs away. It takes a ship six months to get from here to Terra, and another six months to get back. A radio message takes a little over twenty-one years, each way." He holstered the pistol again.

"That brings up another question, general," one of Keaveney's subordinates said. "Can we hold out long enough for help to get here from Terra?"

"By the time help could reach us from Terra," von Schlichten replied, "we'll either have this revolt crushed, or there won't be a live Terran left on Ullr." He felt a brief sadistic pleasure as he watched Keaveney's face sag in horror. "On this planet, there's not more than a three months' supply of any sort of food a human can eat. And the ships that'll be coming in until word of our plight can get to Terra won't bring enough to keep us going. We need the farms and livestock and the animal-tissue culture plant at Konkrook, and the farms at Krink and on the plateau back of Skilk, and we need peace and native labor to work them."

*

Nobody seemed to have anything to say after that, for awhile. Then Keaveney suggested that the next ship was due in from Niflheim in three months, and that it could be used to evacuate all the Terrans on Ullr.

"And I'll personally shoot any able-bodied Terran who tries to board that ship," von Schlichten promised. "Get this through your heads, all of you. We are going to break this rebellion, and we are going to hold Ullr for the Company and the Terran Federation." He looked around him. "Now, get back to work, all of you," he told the group that had formed around him and Keaveney. "Miss Quinton, you just heard me order my adjutant, Colonel O'Leary, on detached duty to Krink. I want you to take over for him. You'll have rank and authority as colonel for the duration of this war."

She was thunderstruck. "But I know absolutely nothing about military matters. There must be a hundred people here who are better qualified than I am...."

"There are, and they all have jobs, and I'd have to find replacements for them, and replacements for the replacements. You won't leave any vacancy to be filled. And you'll learn, fast enough." He went over to the situation-map again, and looked at the arrangements of pink and white pills. "First of all, I want you to call Jarman, at the military airport, and have an airjeep and driver sent around here for me. I'm going up and have a look around. Barney, keep the show going while I'm out, and tell Colonel Quinton what it's all about."

VII

He looked at his watch, as the light airjeep let down into the street. Oh-one-fifteen—two hours and a half since the mutiny at the native-troops barracks had broken out. The Company reservation was still ablaze with lights, and over the roof of the hospital and dispensary and test-lab he could see the glare of the burning barracks. There was more fire-glare to the south, in the direction of the mine-equipment park and the mine-labor camp, and from that direction the bulk of the firing was to be heard.

The driver, a young lieutenant, slid back the duraglass canopy for him to climb in, then snapped it into place when he had strapped himself into his seat, and hit the controls.

They lifted up, the driver turning the nose of the airjeep in the direction of the flames and explosions and magnesium-lights to the south and tapping his booster-button gently. The vehicle shot forward and came floating in over the scene of the fighting. The situation-map at the improvised headquarters had shown a mixture of pink and white pills in the mine-equipment park; something was going to have to be done about the lag in correcting it, for the area was entirely in the hands of loyal Company troops, and the mob of laborers and mutinous soldiers had been pushed back into the temporary camp where the workers had been gathered to await transportation to the Arctic. As he had feared, the rioting workers, many of whom were trained to handle contragravity equipment, had managed to lift up a number of dump-trucks and power-shovels and bulldozers, intending to use them as improvised air-tanks, but Jarman's combat-cars had gotten on the job promptly and all of these had been shot down and were lying in wreckage, mostly among the rows of parked mining-equipment.

*

From the labor-camp, a surprising volume of fire was being directed against the attack which had already started from the retaken equipment-park.

Hovering above the fighting, aloof from it, he saw six long troop-carriers land and disgorge Kragan Rifles who had been released by the liquidation of resistance at the native-troops barracks. A little later, two air-tanks floated in, and then two more, going off contragravity and lumbering forward on treads to fire their 90-mm. rifles. At the same time, combat-cars swooped in, banging away with their lighter auto-cannon and launching rockets. The titanium prefab-huts, set up to house the laborers and intended to be taken north with them for their stay on the polar desert, were simply wiped away. Among the wreckage, resistance was being blown out like the lights of a candelabrum.

He took up the hand-phone and called HQ.

"Von Schlichten; what's the wavelength of the officer in command at the equipment-park?"

A voice at the telecast station furnished it; he punched it out.

"Von Schlichten, right overhead. That you, Major Falkenberg? Nice going, major; how are your casualties?"

"Not too bad. Twenty or thirty Kragans and loyal Skilkans, and eight Terrans killed; about as many wounded."

"Pretty good, considering what you're running into. Get many of your Kragans mounted on those hipposaurs?"

"About a hundred; a lot of 'saurs got shot, while we were leading them out from the stables."

"Well, I can see geeks streaming away from the labor-camp, out the south end, going in the direction of the river. Use what cavalry you have on them, and what contragravity you can spare. I'll drop a few flares to show their position and direction."

Anticipating him, the driver turned the airjeep and started toward the dry Hoork River. Von Schlichten nodded approval and told him to release

53

flares when over the fugitives.

"Right," Falkenberg replied. "I'll get on it at once, general."

"And start moving that mine-equipment up into the Company area. Some of it we can put into the air; the rest we can use to build barricades. None of it do we want the geeks getting hold of, and the equipment-park's outside our practical perimeter. I'll send people to help you move it."

"No need to do that, sir; I have about a hundred and fifty loyal North Ullrans—foremen, technicians, overseers—who can handle it."

"All right. Use your own judgment. Put the stuff back of the native-troops barracks, and between the power-plant and the Company office-buildings, and anywhere else you can." The lieutenant nudged him and pushed a couple of buttons on the dashboard. "Here go the flares, now."

*

Immediately, a couple of airjeeps pounced in, to strafe the fleeing enemy. Somebody must have already been issuing orders on another wavelength; a number of Kragans, riding hipposaurs, were galloping into the light of the flares.

"Now, let's have a look at the native barracks and the maintenance-yards," he said. "And then, we'll make a circuit around the Reservation, about two-three miles out. I'm not happy about where Firkked's army is."

The driver looked at him. "I've been worrying about that, too, sir," he said. "I can't understand why he hasn't jumped us, already. I know it takes time to get one of these geek armies on the road, but...."

"He's hoping our native-troops and the mine laborers will be able to wipe us out, themselves," von Schlichten said.

There was nothing going on in the area between the native barracks and the mountains except some sporadic firing as small patrols of Kragans clashed with clumps of fleeing mutineers. All the barracks, even those of the Rifles, were burning; the red-and-yellow danger-lights around the power-plant and the water-works and the explosives magazines were still on. Most of the floodlights were still on, and there was still some fighting around the maintenance-yard. It looked as though the survivors of the Tenth N.U.N.I. were in a few small pockets which were being squeezed out.

There was nothing at all going on north of the Reservation; the countryside, by day a checkerboard of walled fields and small villages, was dark, except for a dim light, here and there, where the occupants of some farmhouse had been awakened by the noise of battle.

Then, two miles east of the Reservation, he caught a new sound—the flowing, riverlike, murmur of something vast on the move.

"Hear that, lieutenant?" he asked. "Head for it, at about a thousand feet. When we're directly above it, let go some flares."

"Yes, sir." The younger man had lowered his voice to a whisper.

"That's geeks; headed for the Reservation."

"Maybe Firkked's army," von Schlichten thought aloud. "Or maybe a city mob."

*

The noises were growing clearer, louder. He picked up the phone and punched the wavelength of the military airport.

"Von Schlichten; my compliments to Colonel Jarman. Tell him there's a geek mob, or possibly Firkked's regulars, on the main highway from Skilk, two miles east of the Reservation. Get some combat contragravity over here, at once. We'll light them up for you. And tell Colonel Jarman to start flying patrols up and down along the Hoork River; this may not be the only gang that's coming out to see us."

The sounds were directly below, now—the scuffing of horny-soled feet on the dirt road, the clink and rattle of slung weapons, the clicking and squeaking of Ullran voices.

The lieutenant said: "Here go the flares, sir."

Von Schlichten shut his eyes, then opened them slowly. The driver, upon releasing the flares, had nosed up, banked, turned, and was coming in again, down the road toward the advancing column. Von Schlichten peered into his all-armament sight, his foot on the machine-gun pedal and his fingers on the rocket buttons. The highway below was jammed with geeks, and they were all stopped dead and staring upward, as though hypnotized by the lights. It was obviously a mob. A second later, they had recovered and were shooting—not at the airjeep, but at the four globes of blazing magnesium. Then he had the close-packed mass of non-humanity in his sights; he tramped the pedal and began punching buttons. He still had four rockets left by the time the mob was behind him.

"All right, let's take another pass at them. Same direction."

The driver put the airjeep into a quick loop and came out of it in front of the mob, who now had their backs turned and were staring in the direction in which they had last seen the vehicle. Again, von Schlichten plowed them with rockets and harrowed them with his guns. Some of the Skilkans were trying to get over the high fences on either side of the road—really stockades of petrified tree-trunks. Others were firing, and this time they were shooting at the airjeep. It took one hit from a heavy shellosaur-rifle, and immediately the driver banked and turned away from the road, heading back.

"Dammit, why did you do that?" von Schlichten demanded, lifting his foot from the gun-pedal. "Are you afraid of the kind of popguns those geeks are using?"

"I am not afraid to risk my vehicle, or myself, sir," the lieutenant replied, with the extreme formality of a very junior officer chewing out a very senior one. "I am, however, afraid to risk my passenger. Generals are not expendable, sir."

He was right, of course. Von Schlichten admitted it. "I'm too old to play cowboy, like this," he said. "Back to the Reservation; telecast station."

Looking back over his shoulder, he saw eight or ten more flares alight, and the ground-flashes of exploding shells and rockets; the air above the road was sparkling with gun-flames. Jarman must have had some contragravity ready to be sent off on the instant.

*

While he had been out, somebody had gotten a TV-pickup mounted on a contragravity-lifter and run up to two thousand feet, on the end of a steel-tough tensilon mooring-line. The big circular screen was lit, showing the whole Company Reservation, with the surrounding countryside foreshortened by perspective to the distant lights of Skilk. The map had been taken up from the floor, and a big terrain-board had been brought in from the Chief Engineer's office and set up in its place. In front of the screen, Paula Quinton, Barney Mordkovitz, Colonel Cheng-Li, and, conspicuously silent, Jules Keaveney, sat drinking coffee and munching sandwiches. Half a dozen Terrans, of both sexes, were working furiously to get the markers which replaced the pink and white pills placed on the board, and one of Captain Inez Malavez' non-coms, with a headset, was getting combat reports directly from the switchboard. Everything was clicking like well-oiled machinery.

56

On the TV-screen, the Residency area was ablaze with light, and so were the ship-docks, the airport and spaceport, the shops, and the maintenance-yard. On the terrain-board, the latter was now marked as completely in Company hands. The ruins of the native-troops barracks were still burning, and there was a twinkle of orange-red here and there among the ruins of the labor-camp. Much of the equipment for the Polar mines had already been shifted into defensible ground. The rest of the circle was dark, except for the distant lights of Skilk, where the nuclear power plant was apparently still functioning in native hands.

Then, without warning, a spot of white light blazed into being south-east of the Company area and south-west of Skilk, followed by another and another. Instantly, von Schlichten glanced up at the row of smaller screens, and on one of them saw the view as picked up by a patrolling airjeep.

The army of King Firkked of Skilk had finally put in its appearance, about three miles south of the Reservation. The Skilkan regulars had been marching in formation, some on the road and some along parallel lanes and paths. They had the look of trained and disciplined troops, but they had made the same mistake as the rabble that had been shot up on the north side of the Reservation. Unused to attack from the air, they had all halted in place and were gaping open-mouthed, their opal teeth gleaming in the white flare-light.

*

In the big screen, it could be seen that Colonel Jarman had thrown most of his available contragravity at them, including the combat-cars that had already started to form the second wave of the attack on the mob to the north. Other flares bloomed in the darkness, and the fiery trails of rockets curved downward to end in yellow flashes on the ground.

The airjeep with the pickup circled back; the troops on the road and in the adjoining fields had broken. The former were caught between the fences which made Ullran roads such deathtraps when under air-attack. The latter had dispersed, and were running away, individually and by squads; at first, it looked like a panic, but he could see officers signalling to the larger groups of fugitives to open out, apparently directing the flight. By this time, there were ten or twelve combat-cars and about twenty airjeeps at work. In the moving view from the pickup-jeep, he saw what

57

looked like a 90-mm. rocket land in the middle of a company that was still trying to defend itself with small-arms fire on the road, wiping out about half of them.

"The next time they're air-struck, they won't stay bunched," Mordkovitz stated. "A lot of them didn't stay bunched this time, if you noticed. And they'll keep out from between the fences."

In the large screen, a quick succession of gun-flashes leaped up from the direction of the Hoork River; shells began bursting over the scene of the attack. The screen tuned to the pickup on the airjeep went dead; in the big screen, there was a twinkling of falling fire. Almost at once, thirty or forty rocket-trails converged on the gun-position, and, for a moment, explosions burned like a bonfire.

"They had a 75-mm. at the rear of the column," somebody called from the big switchboard. "Lieutenant Kalanang's jeep was hit; Lieutenant Vermaas is cutting in his pickup on the same wavelength."

*

The small screen lighted again. In the big screen, a cluster of magnesium-lights then appeared above where the Skilkan gun had been; in the small screen, there was a stubbled grain-field, pocked with craters, and the bodies of fifteen or twenty natives, all rather badly mangled. An overturned and apparently destroyed 75-mm. gun lay on its side.

"As far as we know, that was the only 75-mm. gun Firkked had," Colonel Cheng-Li said. "He has at least six, possibly ten, 40-mm's. It's a wonder we haven't seen anything of them."

"Well, there's no way of being sure," Jules Keaveney said, "but I have an idea they're all at or around the Palace. Firkked knows about how much contragravity we have. He's probably wondering why we aren't bombing him, now."

"He doesn't know we've sold the Palace to King Jonkvank for an army," von Schlichten said. "And that reminds me; how much contragravity could Firkked scrape together, for an attack on us? I've been expecting a geek Luftwaffe over here, at any moment."

Colonel Cheng-Li studied the smoking tip of his cigarette for a moment. "Well, Firkked owns, personally, three ten-passenger aircars, a thing like a troop-carrier that he transports some of his courtiers around in, four airjeeps armed with a pair of 15-mm. machine-guns apiece, and two big lorries. There are possibly two hundred vehicles of all types in Skilk and the country around, but some of them are in the hands of natives friendly to us."

Von Schlichten nodded. "And there'll be oodles of thermoconcentrate-fuel, and blasting explosives. Colonel Quinton, suppose you call Ed Wallingsby, the Chief Engineer, right away; have him commissioned colonel. Tell him to get to work making this place secure against air-attack, to consult with Colonel Jarman, and to get those geeks Leavitt has penned in the repair-dock at the airport and use them to dig slit-trenches and fill sandbags and so on. He can use Kragan limited-duty wounded to guard them.... Mr. Keaveney, you'll begin setting up something in the way of an ARP-organization. You'll have to get along on what nobody else wants. You will also consult with Colonel Jarman, and with Colonel Wallingsby. Better get started on it now. Just think of everything around here that could go wrong in case of an air attack, and try to do something about it in advance."

VIII

At 0245, an attack developed on the north-western corner of the Reservation, in the direction of the explosives magazines. It turned out to be relatively trivial. Remnants of the mob that had been broken up by air attack on the road had gotten together and were making rushes in small bands, keeping well spread out. Beating them off took considerable ammunition, but it was accomplished with negligible casualties to the defenders. They finally stopped coming around daylight.

In the meantime, Themistocles M'zangwe called from Konkrook. "About six hundred of Kankad's people have gotten in, already, in the damnedest collection of vehicles you ever saw," he reported. "Kankad must be using every scrap of contragravity he has; it's a regular airborne Dunkirk-in-reverse. Kankad sent word that he's coming here in person, as soon as he has things organized at his place. And the geeks, here, have scraped together an air-force of their own—farm-lorries, aircars, that sort of thing—and they're using them to bomb us here and at the mainland farm, mostly with nitroglycerine. We've shot down about twenty of them, but they're still coming. They tried a boat-attack across the Channel. We've been doing some bombing, ourselves; we made a down-payment for Eric

Blount and Hendrik Lemoyne. Took a fifty-ton tank off a fuel-lorry, fitted it with a detonator, filled it with thermoconcentrate, and ferried it over on the Elmoran and dumped it on the Keegarkan Embassy. It must have landed in the middle of the central court; in about fifteen seconds, flames were coming out every window in the place." His face became less jovial. "We had something pretty bad happen here, too," he said. "That Konkrook Fencibles rabble of Prince Jaizerd's mutinied, along with the others; they got into the hospital and butchered everybody in the place, patients and staff. The Kragans got there too late to save anybody, but they wiped out the Fencibles. Jaizerd himself was the only one they took alive, and he didn't stay that way very long."

"How are you making out with your Civil Administration crowd?"

M'zangwe grimaced. "I haven't had to put any of them under actual arrest, so far, but we've had to keep Buhrmann away from the communications equipment by force. He wanted to call you up and chew you out for not evacuating everybody in the North to Konkrook."

"Is he crazy?"

"No, just scared. He says you're going to get everybody on Ullr massacred by detail, when you could save Konkrook by bringing them all here."

"You tell him I'm going to hold this planet, not just one city. Tell him I have a sense of my duty to the Company and its stockholders, if he hasn't; put it in those terms and he may understand you."

*

By 0330, it was daylight; the attacks against the north-west corner of the perimeter stopped entirely. Wallingsby had the three-hundred-odd Skilkan laborers at work; he had gathered up all the tarpaulin he could find, and had the two sewing-machines in the tentmaker's shop running on sandbags. Jules Keaveney, to von Schlichten's agreeable surprise, had taken hold of his ARP assignment, and was doing an efficient job in organizing for fire-fighting, damage-control and first aid. Colonel Jarman had his airjeeps and combat-cars working in ever-widening circles over the countryside, shooting up everything in sight that even looked like contragravity equipment. Some of these patrols had to be recalled, around 1030, when sporadic nuisance-sniping began from the side of the mountain to the west. And, along with everything else, Paula Quinton managed to

60

get a complete digest prepared of the situation elsewhere in the Terran-occupied parts of the planet.

The situation at Konkrook was brightening steadily. The second wave of Kankad's improvised airlift, reenforced by contragravity from Konkrook, had come in; there were now close to two thousand fresh Kragans on Gongonk Island and the mainland farms, Kankad himself with them. The *Aldebaran* had reached Kankad's Town, and was loading another thousand Kragans.... There was nothing more from Keegark. A message from Colonel MacKinnon had come in at dawn, to the effect that the geeks had penetrated his last defenses and that he was about to blow up the Residency; thereafter Keegark went off the air.... By 0730, the *Northern Star* had landed the regiment Murderers, armed with first-quality Terran infantry-rifles and a few machine-guns and bazookas, at the Palace at Krink, and by 0845 she had returned with another regiment, the Jeel-Feeders. The three-street lane connecting the Palace and the Residency had been widened to six, and then to eight.... Guido Karamessinis, at Grank, was still at uneasy peace with King Yoorkerk, who was still undecided whether the rebels or the Company were going to be the eventual victors, and afraid to take any irrevocable step in either direction.

*

At 1100, Paula Quinton and Barney Mordkovitz virtually ordered him to get some sleep. He went to his quarters at Company House, downed a spaceship-captain's-size drink of honey-rum, and slept until 1600. As he dressed and shaved, he could hear, through the open window, the slow sputter of small-arms-fire, punctuated by the occasional *whump-whump-whump* of 40-mm. auto-cannon or the hammering of a machine-gun.

Returning to his command-post at the telecast station, the terrain-board showed that the perimeter of defense had been pushed out in a bulge at the north-west corner; the TV-screen pictured a crude breastwork of petrified tree-trunks, sandbags, mining machinery, packing-cases and odds-and-ends, upon which Wallingsby's native laborers were working under guard while a skirmish-line of Kragans had been thrown out another four or five hundred yards and were exchanging potshots with Skilkans on the gullied hillside.

"Where's Colonel Quinton?" he asked. "She ought to be taking a turn in the sack, now."

ULLR UPRISING

"She's taking one," Major Falkenberg told him. "General Mordkovitz chased her off to bed a couple of hours ago, called me in to take her place, and then went out to replace me. Colonel Guilliford's in the hospital; got hit about thirteen hundred. They're afraid he's going to lose a leg."

More reports came in. The entire garrison of the small Residency at Kwurk, the most northern of the eastern shore Free Cities, had arrived at Kankad's Town in two hundred-foot contragravity scows and five aircars. Two of the aircars arrived half an hour behind the rest of the refugee flotilla, having turned off at Keegark to pay their respects to King Orgzild. They reported the Keegark Residency in ruins, its central buildings vanished in a huge crater; the *Jan Smuts* and the *Christiaan De Wett* were still in the Company docks, both apparently damaged by the blast which had destroyed the Residency. One of the aircars had rocketed and machine-gunned some Keegarkans who appeared to be trying to repair them; the other blew up King Orgzild's nitroglycerine plant. Von Schlichten called Konkrook and ordered a bombing-mission against Keegark organized, to make sure the two ships stayed out of service.

*

The *Northern Star* was still bringing loyal troops into Krink. King Jonkvank, whom von Schlichten called, was highly elated.

"We are killing traitors wherever we find them!" he exulted. "The city is yellow with their blood; their heads are piled everywhere! How is it with you at Skilk? Do the heads fall?"

"We have killed many, also," von Schlichten boasted. "And tonight, we will kill more; we are preparing bombs of great destruction, which we will rain down upon Skilk until there is not one stone left upon another, or one infant of a day's age left alive!"

Jonkvank reacted as he was intended to. "Oh, no, general; don't do all that!" he exclaimed. "You promised me that I should have Skilk, on the word of a Terran. Are you going to give me a city of ruins and corpses? Ruins are no good to anybody, and I am not a Jeel, to eat corpses."

Von Schlichten shrugged. "When you are strong, you can flog your enemies with a whip; when you are weak, all you can do is kill them. If I had five thousand more troops, here...."

"Oh, I will send troops, as soon as I can," Jonkvank hastened to promise. "All my best regiments. But, now that we have stopped this sinful rebellion, here, I can't take chances that it will break out again as soon as I strip the city of troops."

Von Schlichten nodded. Jonkvank's argument made sense; he would have taken a similar position, himself.

"Well, get as many as you can over here, as soon as possible," he said. "We'll try to do as little damage to Skilk as we can, but...."

*

At 1830, Paula joined him for her breakfast, while he sat in front of the big screen, eating his dinner. There had been light ground-action along the southern end of the perimeter—King Firkked's regulars, reinforced by Zirk tribesmen and levies of townspeople, all of whom seemed to have firearms, were filtering in through the ruins of the labor-camp and the wreckage of the equipment-park—and there was renewed sniping from the mountainside. The long afternoon of the northern Autumn dragged on; finally, at 2200, the sun set, and it was not fully dark for another hour. For some time, there was an ominous quiet, and then, at 0030, the enemy began attacking in force, driving herds of livestock—lumbering six-legged brutes bred by the North Ullrans for food—to test the defenses for electrified wire and landmines. Most of these were shot down or blown up, but a few got as far as the wire, which, by now, had been strung and electrified completely around the perimeter.

Behind them came parties of Skilkan regulars with long-handled insulated cutters; a couple of cuts were made in the wire, and a section of it went dead. The line, at this point, had been rather thinly held; the defenders immediately called for air-support, and Jarman ordered fifteen of his remaining twenty airjeeps and five combat-cars into the fight. No sooner were they committed than the radar on the commercial airport control-tower picked up air vehicles approaching from the north, and the air-raid sirens began howling and the searchlights went on.

The contragravity which had been sent to support the ground-defense at the south side of the Reservation turned to meet this new threat, and everything else available, including the four heavy air-tanks, lifted up. Meanwhile, guns began firing from the ground and from rooftops.

There had been four aircars, ordinary passenger vehicles equipped with machine-guns on improvised mounts, and ten big lorries converted into bombers, in the attack. All the lorries, and all but one of the makeshift fighter-escort, were shot down, but not before explosive and thermoconcentrate bombs were dumped all over the place. One lorry emptied its load of thermoconcentrate-bombs on the control-building at the airport, starting a raging fire and putting the radar out of commission. A repair-shop at ordnance-depot was set on fire, and a quantity of small-arms and machine-gun ammunition piled outside for transportation to the outer defenses blew up. An explosive bomb landed on the roof of the building between Company House and the telecast station, blowing a hole in the roof and demolishing the upper floor. And another load of thermoconcentrate, missing the power-plant, set fire to the dry grass between it and the ruins of the native-troops barracks.

*

Before the air-attack had been broken up, the soldiers of King Firkked and their irregular supporters were swarming through the dead section of wire. They had four or five big farm-tractors, nuclear-powered but unequipped with contragravity-generators, which they were using like ground-tanks of the First Century. This attack penetrated to the middle of the Reservation before it was stopped and the attackers either killed or driven out; for the first time since daybreak, the red-and-yellow lights came on around the power-plant.

As soon as the combined air and ground attack was beaten off, von Schlichten ordered all his available contragravity up, flying patrols around the Reservation and retaliatory bombing missions against Skilk, and began bombarding the city with his 90-mm. guns. A number of fires broke out, and at about 0200 a huge expanding globe of orange-red flame soared up from the city.

"There goes Firkked's thermoconcentrate stock," he said to Paula, who was standing beside him in front of the screen.

Half an hour later, he discovered that he had been over-optimistic. Much of the enemy's supply of Terran thermoconcentrate had been destroyed, but enough remained to pelt the Reservation and the Company buildings with incendiaries, when a second and more severe air-attack developed, consisting of forty or fifty makeshift lorry-bombers and fifteen aircars.

Like the first, the second air-attack was beaten off, or, more exactly, down. Most of the enemy contragravity was destroyed; at least two dozen vehicles crashed inside the Reservation. As in the first instance, there was a simultaneous ground attack from the southern side, with a demonstration-attack at the north end. It was full daylight before the last of the attackers was either killed or driven out.

Five minutes later, the *Northern Star* came bulking over the mountains from the west.

IX

Von Schlichten raced for the telecast station, to receive a call from a Colonel Khalid ib'n Talal, aboard the approaching ship.

"I've one of Jonkvank's regiments, the Jeel-Feeders, armed with Terran 9-mm. rifles and a few bazookas; I have a company of our Zirks, with their mounts, and a battalion of the Sixth N.U.N.I.; I also have four 90-mm. guns, Terran-manned," he reported. "What's the situation, general, and where do you want me to land?"

Von Schlichten described the situation succinctly, in an ancient and unprintable military cliche. "Try landing south of the Reservation, a little west of the ruins of the labor-camp," he advised. "The bulk of Firkked's army is in that section, and I want them run out as soon as possible. We'll give you all the contragravity and fire support we can."

The *Northern Star* let down slowly, firing her guns and dropping bombs; as she descended, rifle-fire spurted from all her lower-deck portholes. There was cheering, human and Ullran, from inside the battered defense-perimeter; combat-cars, airjeeps, and improvised bombers lifted out to strafe the Skilkans on the ground, and the four air-tanks moved out to take position and open fire with their 90-mm.'s, helping to flush King Firkked's regulars and auxiliaries out of the gullies and ruins and drive them south along the mountain, away from where the ship would land and also away from the city of Skilk. The *Northern Star* set down quickly, and troops and artillery began to be unloaded, joining in the fighting.

It was five hundred miles to Krink; three hours after lifting out, the *Northern Star* was back again, with two more of King Jonkvank's infantry regiments, and by 1300, when the fourth load arrived from Krink, the fighting was entirely on the eastern bank of the dry Hoork River. This last contingent of reenforcements was landed in the eastern suburbs of Skilk and began fighting their way into the city from the rear.

ULLR UPRISING

It was evident, however, that the pacification of Skilk would not be accomplished as rapidly as von Schlichten wished—street fighting, against a determined enemy, is notoriously slow work—and he decided to risk the *Northern Star* in an attack against the Palace itself, and, over the objections of Paula Quinton, Jules Keaveney, and Barney Mordkovitz, to lead the attack in person.

*

Inside the city, he found that the Zirk cavalry from Krink had thrust up one of the broader streets to within a thousand yards of the Palace, and, supported by infantry, contragravity, and a couple of air-tanks, were pounding and hacking at a mass of Skilkans whose uniform lack of costume prevented distinguishing between soldiery and townsfolk. Very few of these, he observed, seemed to be using firearms; with his glasses, he could see them shooting with long Northern air-rifles and a few Takkad Sea crossbows. Either weapon would shoot clear through a Terran or half-way through an Ullran at fifty yards, but at over two hundred they were almost harmless. There were a few fires still burning from the bombardment of the night before—Ullran, and particularly North Ullran, cities did not burn well—and the blaze which had consumed the bulk of Firkked's stock of thermoconcentrate fuel had long ago burned out, leaving an area of six or eight blocks blackened and lifeless.

The ship let down, while the six combat-cars which had accompanied her buzzed the Palace roof, strafing it to keep it clear, and the Kragans aboard fired with their rifles. She came to rest on seven-eights weight reduction, and even before the gangplanks were run out, the Kragans were dropping to the flat roof, running to stairhead penthouses and tossing grenades into them.

The taking of the Palace was a gruesome business. Knowing exactly how much mercy they would have shown had they been storming the Residency, Firkked's soldiers and courtiers fought desperately and had to be exterminated, floor by floor, room by room, hallway by hallway. They had to fight for every inch downward.

Driving down from above, von Schlichten and his Kragans slithered over floors increasingly greasy with yellow Ullran blood. He had picked up a broadsword at the foot of the first stairway down; a little later, he tossed it aside in favor of another, better balanced and with a better guard. There was a furious battle at the doorways of the Throne Room; finally, climbing over the bodies of their own dead and the enemy's, they were inside.

*

Here there was no question of quarter whatever, at least as long as Firkked lived; North Ullran nobles did not surrender under the eyes of their king, and North Ullran kings did not surrender their thrones alive. There was also a tradition, of which von Schlichten was mindful, that a king must only be killed by his conqueror, in personal combat, with steel.

With a wedge of Kragan bayonets around him and the picked-up broadsword in his hand, he fought his way to the throne, where Firkked waited, a sword in one of his upper hands, his Spear of State in the other, and a dagger in either lower hand. With his left hand, von Schlichten detached the bayonet from the rifle of one of his followers and went forward, trying not to think of the absurdity of a man of the Sixth Century A.E., the representative of a civilized Chartered Company, dueling to the death with swords with a barbarian king for a throne he had promised to another barbarian, or of what could happen on Ullr if he allowed this four-armed monstrosity to kill him.

It was not as bad as it looked, however. The ornate Spear of State, in spite of its long, cruel-looking blade, was not an especially good combat-weapon, at least for one hand, and Firkked seemed confused by the very abundance of his armament. After a few slashes and jabs, von Schlichten knocked the unwieldy thing from his opponent's hand. This raised a fearful ullulation from the Skilkan nobility, who had stopped fighting to watch the duel; evidently it was the very worst sort of a bad omen. Firkked, seemingly relieved to be disencumbered of the thing, caught his sword in both hands and aimed a roundhouse swing at von Schlichten's head; von Schlichten dodged, crippled one of Firkked's lower hands with a quick slash, and lunged at the royal belly. Firkked used his remaining dagger to parry, backed a step closer his throne, and took another swing with his sword, which von Schlichten parried on the bayonet in his left hand. Then, backing, he slashed at the inside of Firkked's leg with the thousand-year-old *coup-de-Jarnac*. Firkked, unable to support the weight of his dense-tissued body on one leg, stumbled; von Schlichten ran him neatly through the breast with his sword and through the throat with the bayonet.

There was silence in the throne-room for an instant, and then, with a horrible collective shriek, the Skilkans threw down their weapons. One of von Schlichten's Kragans slung his rifle and picked up the Spear of State with all four hands, taking his post ceremoniously behind the victor. A couple of others dragged the body of Firkked to the edge of the dais, and one of them drew his leaf-shaped short-sword and beheaded it.

At mid-afternoon, von Schlichten was on the roof of the Palace, holding the Spear of State, with Firkked's head impaled on the point, while a Terran technician aimed an audio-visual recorder.

"This," he said, with the geek-speaker in his mouth, "is King Firkked's Spear of State, and here, upon it, is King Firkked's head. Two days ago, Firkked was at peace with the Company, and Firkked was King in Skilk. If he had not dared raise his feeble hand against the might of the Ullr Company, he would still be alive, and his Spear would still be borne behind him. So must all those who rise against the Company perish.... Cut."

The camera stopped. A Kragan came forward and took the Spear of State, with its grisly burden, carrying it to a nearby wall and leaning it up, like a piece of stage property no longer required for this scene but needed for the next. Von Schlichten took out his geek-speaker, wiped and pouched it, and took his cigarette case from his pocket.

"Well, this is the limit!" Paula Quinton, who had come up during the filming of the scene, exploded. "I thought you had to kill him yourself in order to encourage your soldiers; I didn't think you wanted to make a movie of it to show your friends."

Von Schlichten tapped the cigarette on the gold-and-platinum case and stared at her through his monocle.

"Sit down, colonel." He lit the cigarette. "Your politico-military education still needs a little filling in. At Grank, we have two ships. One is the *Northern Lights*, sister ships of the *Northern Star*. The other is the cruiser *Procyon*, the only real warship on Ullr, with a main battery of four 200-mm. guns. How King Yoorkerk was able to get control of those ships I don't know, but there will be a board of inquiry and maybe a couple of courts-martial, when things get stabilized to a point where we can afford such luxuries. As it is, we need those ships desperately, and as soon as he gets in, I'm sending Hideyoshi O'Leary to Grank with the *Northern Star* and a load of Kragan Rifles, to pry them loose. The audio-visual of which this is the last scene is going to be one of the crowbars he's going to use."

"But why did you have to fight Firkked, yourself?" she asked.

"I had to kill him, myself, with a sword; according to local custom, that makes me King of Skilk."

"Why, your Majesty!" She rose and curtsied mockingly. "But I thought you were going to make Jonkvank King of Skilk."

He shook his head. "Just Viceroy," he corrected. "I'm handing the Spear of State *down* to him, not up to him; he'll reign as my vassal, and, consequently, as vassal of the Company, and before long, he won't be much more at Krink, either. That'll take a little longer—there'll have to be military missions, and economic missions, and trade-agreements, and all the rest of it, first—but he's on the way to becoming a puppet-prince."

*

Half an hour later, a large and excessively ornate air-launch, specially built at the Konkrook shipyards for King Jonkvank, was sighted coming over the mountain from the east. An escort of combat-cars was sent to meet it, and a battalion of Kragans and the survivors of Firkked's court were drawn up on the Palace roof.

"His Majesty, Jonkvank, King of Krink!" the former herald of King Firkked's court, now herald to King Carlos von Schlichten, shouted, banging on a brass shield with the flat of his sword, as Jonkvank descended from his launch, attended by a group of his nobles and his Spear of State, with Hideyoshi O'Leary and Francis X. Shapiro shepherding them. As the guests advanced across the roof, the herald banged again on his shield.

"His Majesty, Carlos von Schlichten,"—which came out more or less as Karlok vonk Zlikdenk—"King, by right of combat, of Skilk!"

Von Schlichten advanced to meet his fellow-monarch, his own Spear of State, with Firkked's head still grinning from it, two paces behind him.

Jonkvank stopped, his face contorted with saurian rage.

"What is this?" he demanded. "You told me that I could be King of Skilk; is this how a Terran keeps his word?"

"A Terran's word is always good, Jonkvank," von Schlichten replied, omitting the titles, as was proper in one sovereign addressing another. "My word was that you should reign in Skilk, and my word stands. But these things must be done decently, according to custom and law. I killed

69

Firkked in single combat. Had I not done so, the Spear of Skilk would have been left lying, for any of the young of Firkked to pick up. Is that not the law?"

Jonkvank nodded grudgingly. "It is the law," he admitted.

"Good. Now, since I killed Firkked in lawful manner, his Spear is mine, and what is mine I can give as I please. I now give you the Spear of Skilk, to carry in my name, as I promised."

The Kragan who was carrying the ceremonial weapon tossed the head of Firkked from the point; another Kragan kicked it aside and advanced to wipe the spear-blade with a rag. Von Schlichten took the spear and gave it to Jonkvank.

"This is not good!" one of the Skilkan nobles protested. "That you should rule over us, yes. You killed Firkked in single combat, and you are the soldier of the Company, which is mighty, as all here have seen. But that this foreigner be given the Spear of Skilk, that is not at all good!"

Some of the others, emboldened by his example, were jabbering agreement.

"Listen, all of you!" von Schlichten shouted. "Here is no question of Krink ruling over Skilk. Does it matter who holds the Spear of Skilk, when he does so in my name? And King Jonkvank will be no foreigner. He will come and live among you, and later he will travel back and forth between Krink and Skilk, and he will leave the Spear of Krink in Krink, and the Spear of Skilk in Skilk, and in Skilk he will be a Skilkan. That is how it must be."

*

That seemed to satisfy everybody except Jonkvank, and he had wit enough not to make an issue of it. He even had the Spear of Krink carried back aboard his launch, out of sight, and when he accompanied von Schlichten, an hour later, to see Hideyoshi O'Leary off for Grank, he had the Spear of Skilk carried behind him. When he was alone with von Schlichten, in the room that had been King Firkked's bedchamber, however, he exploded.

"What is all this foolishness which you promised these people in my name and which I must now carry out? That I am to leave the Spear of Skilk in Skilk and the Spear of Krink in Krink, and come here to live...."

"You wish to hold Skilk?" von Schlichten asked.

"I intend to hold Skilk. To begin with, there shall be a great killing here. A very great killing: of all those who advised that fool of a Firkked to start this business; of those who gave shelter to the false prophet, Rakkeed, when he was here; of the faithless priests who gave ear to his abominable heresies and allowed him to spew out his blasphemies in the temples; of those who sent spies to Krink, to corrupt and pervert my soldiers and nobles; of those who...."

"All that is as it should be," von Schlichten agreed. "Except that it must be done quickly and all at once, before the memories of these crimes fade from the minds of the people. And great care must be taken to kill only those who can be proven to be guilty of something; thus it will be said that the justice of King Jonkvank is terrible to evildoers but a protection and a shield to those who keep the peace and obey the laws. And when the priests are to be killed, it should be done under the direction of those other priests who were faithful to the gods and whom King Firkked drove out of their temples, and it must be done in the name of the gods. Thus will you be esteemed a pious, and not an impious, king. It must not be allowed to seem that the city has come under foreign rule. And you must not change the laws, unless the people petition you to do so, nor must you increase the taxes, and you must not confiscate the estates of those who are put to death, for the death of parents is always forgiven before the loss of patrimonies. And you should select certain Skilkan nobles, and become the father of their young, and above all, you must leave none of the young of Firkked alive, to raise rebellion against you later."

Jonkvank nodded, deeply impressed. "By the gods, Karlok vonk Zlikdenk, this is wisdom! Now it is to be seen why the likes of Firkked cannot prevail against you, or against the Company as long as you are the Company's upper sword-arm!"

Honesty tempted von Schlichten, for a moment, to disclaim originality for the principles he had just enunciated, even at the price of trying to pronounce the name of Niccolo Machiavelli with a geek-speaker.

*

The sun slid lower and lower toward the horizon behind them as the aircar bulleted south along the broad valley and dry bed of the Hoork River, nearing the zone of equal day and night. Hassan Bogdanoff drove while Harry Quong finished his lunch, then changed places to begin his

71

own. Von Schlichten got two bottles of beer from the refrigerated section of the lunch-hamper and opened one for Paula Quinton and one for himself.

"What are we going to do with these geeks,"—she was using the nasty and derogatory word unconsciously and by custom, now—"after this is all over? We can't just tell them, 'Jolly well played; nice game, wasn't it?' and go back to where we were Wednesday evening."

"No, we can't. There's going to have to be a Terran seizure of political power in every part of this planet that we occupy, and as soon as we're consolidated around the north of Takkad Sea, we're going to have to move in elsewhere," he replied. "Keegark, Konkrook, and the Free Cities, of course, will be relatively easy. They're in arms against us now, and we can take them over by force. We had to make that deal with Jonkvank, or, rather, I did, so that will be a slower process, but we'll get it done in time. If I know that pair as well as I think I do, Jonkvank and Yoorkerk will give us plenty of pretexts, before long. Then, we can start giving them government by law instead of by royal decree, and real courts of justice; put an end to the head-payment system, and to these arbitrary mass arrests and tax-delinquency imprisonments that are nothing but slave-raids by the geek princes on their own people. And, gradually, abolish serfdom. In a couple of centuries, this planet will be fit to admit to the Federation, like Odin and Freya."

"Well, won't that depend a lot on whom the Company sends here to take Harrington's place?"

"Unless I'm much mistaken, the Company will confirm me," he replied. "Administration on Ullr is going to be a military matter for a long time to come, and even the Banking Cartel and the mercantile interests in the Company are going to realize that, and see the necessity for taking political control. And just to make sure, I'm sending Hid O'Leary to Terra on the next ship, to make a full report on the situation."

"You think it'll be cleared up by then? The *City of Montevideo* is due in from Niflheim in a little under three months."

"It'll have to be cleared up by then. We can't keep this war going more than a month, at the present rate. Police-action, and mopping-up, yes; full-scale war, no."

"Ammunition?" she asked.

*

He looked at her in pleased surprise. "Your education has been progressing, at that," he said. "You know, a lot of professional officers, even up to field rank in the combat branches, seem to think that ammo comes down miraculously from Heaven, in contragravity lorries, every time they pray into a radio for it. It doesn't; it has to be produced as fast as it's expended, and we haven't been doing that. So we'll have to lick these geeks before it runs out, because we can't lick them with gun-butts and bayonets."

"Well, how about nuclear weapons?" Paula asked. "I hate to suggest it—I know what they did on Mimir, and Fenris, and Midgard, and what they did on Terra, during the First Century. But it may be our only chance."

He finished his beer and shoved the bottle into the waste-receiver, then got out his cigarettes. "There isn't a single nuclear bomb on the planet. The Company's always refused to allow them to be manufactured or stockpiled here."

"I don't think there'd be any criticism of your making them, now, general. And there's certainly plenty of plutonium. You could make A-bombs, at least."

"There isn't anybody here who even knows how to make one. Most of our nuclear engineers could work one up, in about three months, when we'd either not need one or not be alive."

"Dr. Gomes, who came in on the *Pretoria*, two weeks ago, can make them," she contradicted. "He built at, least a dozen of them on Niflheim, to use in activating volcanoes and bringing ore-bearing lava to the surface."

Von Schlichten's hand, bringing his lighter to the tip of his cigarette, paused for a second. Then he completed the operation, snapped it shut, and put it away.

"When did all this happen?"

She took time out for mental arithmetic; even a spaceship officer had to do that, when a question of interstellar time-relations arose.

"About three-fifty days ago, Galactic Standard. They'd put off the first shot, six bombs, before I got in from Terra. I saw the second shot a day or so before I left Niflheim on the *Canberra*. Dr. Gomes had to stay over till the *Pretoria* to put off the third shot. Why?"

"Did you run into a geek named Gorkrink, while you were on Nif?" he asked her. "And what sort of work was he doing?"

*

"Gorkrink? I don't seem to remember.... Oh, yes! He was helping Dr. Murillo, the seismologist. His year was up after the second shot; he came to Ullr on the *Canberra*. Dr. Murillo was sorry to lose him. He understood Lingua Terra perfectly; Dr. Murillo could talk to him, the way you do with Kankad, without using a geek-speaker."

"Well, but what sort of work ...?"

"Helping set and fire the A-bombs.... *Oh! Good Lord!*"

"You can say that again, and deal in Allah, Shiva, and Kali," von Schlichten told her. "Especially Kali.... Harry! See if you can get some more speed out of this can. I want to get to Konkrook while it's still there!"

It wouldn't be there long, the way things looked. King Orgzild had four tons of plutonium, and with Prince Gorkrink probably able to build A-bombs, Keegark would be set to bring Ullr its first taste of nuclear warfare. Von Schlichten shuddered as he pictured that happening. At the moment, shuddering was about the only thing he could do.

X

It was full dark when Konkrook came in view beyond the East Konk Mountains, a lurid smear on the underside of the clouds, and at Gongonk Island and at the Company farms to the south, a couple of bunches of searchlights were fingering about in the sky. When von Schlichten turned on the outside sound-pickup, he could hear the distant tom-tomming of heavy guns, and the crash of shells and bombs. Keeping the car high enough to be above the trajectories of incoming shells, Harry Quong circled over the city while Hassan Bogdanoff talked to Gongonk Inland on the radio.

The city was in a bad way. There were seventy-five to a hundred big fires going, and a new one started in a rising ball of thermoconcentrate flame while they watched. The three gun-cutters, *Elmoran*, *Gaucho* and *Bushranger*, and about fifty big freight lorries converted to bombers, were shuttling back and forth between the island and the city. The Royal Palace was on fire from end to end, and the entire waterfront and industrial district were in flames. Combat-cars and air jeeps were diving in to shell and rocket and machine-gun streets and buildings. He saw six big bomber-lorries move in dignified procession to unload, one after the other, on a row of buildings along what the Terrans called South Tenth Street, and on the roofs of buildings a block away, red and blue flares were burning, and he could see figures, both human and Ullran, setting up mortars and machine-guns.

Landing on the top stage of Company House, on the island, they were met by a Terran whom von Schlichten had seen, a few days ago, bossing native labor at the spaceport, but who was now wearing a major's insignia. He greeted von Schlichten with a salute which he must have learned from some movie about the ancient French Foreign Legion. Von Schlichten seriously returned it in kind.

"Everybody's down in the Governor-General's office, sir," he said. "Your office, that is. King Kankad's here with us, too."

He accompanied them to the elevator, then turned to a telephone; when von Schlichten and Paula reached the office, everybody was crowded at the door to greet them: Themistocles M'zangwe, his arm in a sling; Hans Meyerstein, the Johannesburg lawyer, who seemed to have even more Bantu blood than the brigadier-general; Morton Buhrmann, the Commercial Superintendent; Laviola, the Fiscal Secretary; a dozen or so other officers and civil administrators. There was a hubbub of greetings, and he was pleased to detect as much real warmth from the civil administration crowd as from the officers.

"Well, I'm glad to be back with you," he replied, generally. "And let me present Colonel Paula Quinton, my new adjutant; Hideyoshi O'Leary's on duty in the North.... Them, this was a perfectly splendid piece of work, here; you can take this not only as a personal congratulation, but as a sort of unit citation for the whole crowd. You've all behaved above praise." He turned to King Kankad, who was wearing a pair of automatics in shoulder-holsters for his upper hands and another pair in cross-body belt holsters for his lower. "And what I've said for anybody else goes double for you, Kankad," he added, clapping the Kragan on the shoulder.

"All he did was save the lot of us!" M'zangwe said. "We were hanging on by our fingernails here till his people started coming in. And then, after you sent the *Aldebaran*...."

"Where is the *Aldebaran*, by the way? I didn't see her when I came in."

"Based on Kankad's, flying bombardment against Keegark, and keeping an eye out for those ships. Prinsloo caught the *De Wett* in the docks there and smashed her, but the *Jan Smuts* got away, and we haven't been able to locate the *Oom Paul Kruger*, either. They're probably both on the Eastern Shore, gathering up reenforcements for Orgzild," M'zangwe said.

"Our ability to move troops rapidly is what's kept us on top this long, and Orgzild's had plenty of time to realize it," von Schlichten said. "When we get *Procyon* down here, I'm going to send her out, with a screen of light scout-vehicles, to find those ships and get rid of them.... How's Hid been making out, at Grank, by the way? I didn't have my car-radio on, coming down."

That touched off another hubbub: "Haven't you heard, general?" ... "Oh, my God, this is simply out of this continuum!" ... "Well, tell him, somebody!" ... "No, get Hid on the screen; it's his story!"

Somebody busied himself at the switchboard. The rest of them sat down at the long conference-table. Laviola and Meyerstein and Buhrmann were especially obsequious in seating von Schlichten in Sid Harrington's old chair, and in getting a chair for Paula Quinton. After awhile, the jumbled colors on the big screen resolved themselves into an image of Hideyoshi O'Leary, grinning like a pussycat beside an empty goldfish-bowl, licking its chops.

"Well, what happened?" von Schlichten asked, after they had exchanged greetings. "How did Yoorkerk like the movies? And did you get the *Procyon* and the *Northern Lights* loose?"

"Yoorkerk was deeply impressed," O'Leary replied. "His story is that he is and always was the true and ever-loving friend of the Company; he acted to prevent quote certain disloyal elements unquote from harming the people and property of the Company. *Procyon's* on the way to Konkrook. I'm holding *Northern Lights* here and *Northern Star* at Skilk; where do you want them sent?"

"Leave *Northern Star* at Skilk, for the time being. Tell the Company's great and good friend King Yoorkerk that the Company expects him to contribute some soldiers for the campaign here and against Keegark, when that starts; be sure you get the best-armed and best-trained regiments he has, and get them down here as soon as possible. Don't send any of your

Kragans or Karamessinis' troops here, though; hold them in Grank till we make sure of the quality of Yoorkerk's friendship."

"Well, general, I think we can be pretty sure, now. You see, he turned Rakkeed the Prophet over to me...."

"*What?*" Von Schlichten felt his monocle starting to slip and took a firmer grip on it. "Who?"

"Pay me, Them; he didn't drop it," Hideyoshi O'Leary said. "Why, Rakkeed the Prophet. Yoorkerk was holding our ships and our people in case we lost; he was also holding Rakkeed at the Palace in case we won. Of course, Rakkeed thought he was an honored guest, right up till Yoorkerk's guards dragged him in and turned him over to us...."

"That geek," von Schlichten said, "is too smart for his own good. Some of these days he's going to play both ends against the middle and both ends'll fold in on him and smash him." A suspicion occurred to him. "You sure this is Rakkeed? It would be just like Yoorkerk to try to sell us a ringer."

O'Leary shook his head solemnly. "I thought of that, right away. This is the real article; Karamessinis' Constabulary and Intelligence officers certified him for me. What do you want me to do, send him down to Konkrook?"

Von Schlichten shook his head. "Get the priests of the locally venerated gods to put him on trial for blasphemy, heresy, impersonating a prophet, practicing witchcraft without a license, or any other ecclesiastical crimes you or they can think of. Then, after he's been given a scrupulously fair trial, have the soldiers of King Yoorkerk behead him, and stick his head up over a big sign, in all native languages, 'Rakkeed the False Prophet.' And have audio-visuals made of the whole business, trial and execution, and be sure that the priests and Yoorkerk's officers are in the foreground and our people stay out of the pictures."

"Soap and towels, for General Pontius von Pilate!" Paula Quinton called out.

"That's an idea; I was wondering what to give Yoorkerk as a testimonial present," Hideyoshi O'Leary said. "A nice thirty-piece silver set!"

"Quite appropriate," von Schlichten approved. "Well, you did a first-class job. I want you back with us as soon as possible—incidentally, you're now a brigadier-general—but not till the situation Grank-Krink-Skilk is stabilized. And, eventually, you'll probably have to set up permanent headquarters in the North."

*

After Hideyoshi O'Leary had thanked him and signed off, and the screen was dark again, he turned to the others.

"Well, gentlemen, I don't think we need worry too much about the North, for the next few days. How long do you estimate this operation against Konkrook's going to take, to complete pacification, Them?"

"How complete is complete pacification, general?" Themistocles M'zangwe wanted to know. "If you mean to the end of organized resistance by larger than squad-size groups, I'd say three days, give or take twelve hours. Of course, there'll be small groups holding out for a couple of weeks, particularly in the farming country and back in the forest...."

"We can forget them; that's minor-tactics stuff. We'll need to keep some kind of an occupation force here for some time; they can deal with that. We'll have to get to work on Keegark, as soon as possible; after we've reduced Keegark, we'll be able to reorganize for a campaign against the Free Cities on the Eastern Shore."

"Begging your pardon, general, but reduce is a mild word for what we ought to do to Keegark," Hans Meyerstein said. "We ought to raze that city as flat as a football field, and then play football on it with King Orgzild's head."

"Any special reason?" von Schlichten asked. "In addition to the Blount-Lemoyne massacre, that is?"

"I should say so, general!" Themistocles M'zangwe backed Meyerstein up. "Bob, you tell him."

Colonel Robert Grinell, the Intelligence officer, got up and took the cigar out of his mouth. He was short and round-bodied and bald-headed, but he was old Terran Federation Regular Army through and through.

"Well, general, we've been finding out quite a bit about the genesis of this business, lately," he said. "From up North, it probably looked like an all-Rakkeed show; that's how it was supposed to look. But the whole thing was hatched at Keegark, by King Orgzild. We've managed to capture a few prominent Konkrookans"—he named half a dozen—"who've been made to talk, and a number of others have come in voluntarily and furnished information. Orgzild conceived the scheme in the beginning; Rakkeed was just the messenger-boy. My face gets the color of the Company trademark every time I think that the whole thing was planned for over a year, right under our noses, even to the signal that was to touch the whole thing off...."

"The poisoning of Sid Harrington, and our announcement of his death?" von Schlichten asked.

"You figured that out yourself, sir? Well, that was most of it."

Grinell went on to elaborate, while von Schlichten tried to keep the impatience out of his face. Beside him, Paula Quinton was fidgeting, too; she was thinking, as he was, of what King Orgzild and Prince Gorkrink were doing now. "And I know positively that the order for the poisoning of Sid Harrington came from the Keegarkan Embassy, here, and was passed down through Gurgurk and Keeluk to this geek here who actually put the poison in the whiskey."

"Yes. I agree that Keegark should be wiped out, and I'd like to have an immediate estimate on the time it'll take to build a nuclear bomb to do the job. One of the old-fashioned plutonium fission A-bombs will do quite well."

Everybody turned quickly. There was a momentary silence, and then Colonel Evan Colbert, of the Fourth Kragan Rifles, the senior officer under Themistocles M'zangwe, found his voice.

"If that's an order, general, we'll get it done. But I'd like to remind you, first, of the Company policy on nuclear weapons on this planet."

"I'm aware of that policy. I'm also aware of the reason for it. We've been compelled, because of the lack of natural fuel on Ullr, to set up nuclear power reactors and furnish large quantities of plutonium to the geeks to fuel them. The Company doesn't want the natives here learning of the possibility of using nuclear energy for destructive purposes. Well, gentlemen, that's a dead issue. They've learned it, thanks to our people on Niflheim, and unless my estimate is entirely wrong, King Orgzild already has at least one First-Century Nagasaki-type plutonium bomb. I am inclined to believe that he had at least one such bomb, probably more, at the time when orders were sent to his embassy, here, for the poisoning of Governor-General Harrington."

With that, he selected a cigarette from his case, offered it to Paula, and snapped his lighter. She had hers lit, and he was puffing on his own, when the others finally realized what he had told them.

"That's impossible!" somebody down the table shouted, as though that would make it so. Another—one of the civil administration crowd—almost exactly repeated Jules Keaveney's words at Skilk: "What the hell was Intelligence doing; sleeping?"

"General von Schlichten," Colonel Grinell took oblique cognizance of the question. "You've just made, by implication, a most grave charge against my department. If you're not mistaken in what you've just said, I deserve to be court-martialled."

"I couldn't bring charges against you, colonel; if it were a court-martial matter, I'd belong in the dock with you," von Schlichten told him. "It seems, though, that a piece of vital information was possessed by those who were unable to evaluate it, and until this afternoon, I was ignorant of its existence. Colonel Quinton, suppose you repeat what you told me, on the way down from Skilk."

"Well, general, don't you think we ought to have Dr. Gomes do that?" Paula asked. "After all, he constructed those bombs on Niflheim, and it'll be he who'll have to build ours."

*

Von Schlichten nodded in instant agreement.

"That's right." He looked around. "Where's Dr. Lourenço Gomes, the nuclear engineer who came in on the *Pretoria*, two weeks ago? Send out for him, and get him in here to me at once."

There was another awkward silence. Then Kent Pickering, the chief of the Gongonk Island power-plant, cleared his throat.

"Why, general, didn't you know? Dr. Gomes is dead. He was killed during the first half hour of the uprising."

XI

He flinched inwardly, and tightened his eye-muscles on the edge of the monocle to keep them from flinching physically as well, trying to freeze out of his face the consternation he felt.

"That's bad, Kent," he said. "Very bad. I'd been counting heavily on Dr. Gomes to design a bomb of our own."

"Well, general, if you please." That was Air-Commodore Leslie Hargreaves. "You say you suspect that King Orgzild has developed a nuclear bomb. If that's true, it's a horrible danger to all of us. But I find it hard to believe that the Keegarkans could have done so, with their resources and at their technological level. Now, if it had been the Kragans, that would have been different, but...."

"Paula, you'd better carry on and explain what you told me, and add anything else you can think of that might be relevant.... Is that sound-recorder turned on? Then turn it on, somebody; we want this taped."

*

Paula rose and began talking: "I suppose you all understand what conditions are on Niflheim, and how these Ullran native workers are employed; however, I'd better begin by explaining the purpose for which these nuclear bombs were designed and used...."

He smiled; she realized that he needed time to think, and she was stalling to provide it. He drew a pencil and pad toward him and began doodling in a bored manner, deliberately closing his mind to what she was saying. There were two assumptions, he considered: first, that King Orgzild already possessed a nuclear bomb which he could use when he chose, and, second, that in the absence of Dr. Gomes, such a bomb could only be produced on Gongonk Island after lengthy experimental work. If both of these assumptions were true, he had just heard the death-sentence of every Terran on Ullr. The first he did not for a moment doubt. The reasons for making it were too good. He dismissed it from further consideration and concentrated on the second.

"... what's known as a Nagasaki-type bomb, the first type of plutonium-bomb developed," Paula was saying. "Really, it's a technological antique, but it was good enough for the purpose, and Dr. Gomes could build it with locally available materials...."

That was the crux of it. The plutonium bomb, from a military standpoint, was as obsolete as the flintlock musket had been at the time of the Second World War. He reviewed, quickly, the history of weapons-development since the beginning of the Atomic Era. The emphasis, since the end of the Second World War, had all been on nuclear weapons and rocket-missiles. There had been the H-bomb, itself obsolescent, and the Bethe-cycle bomb, and the subneutron bomb, and the omega-ray bomb, and the negamatter bomb, and then the end of civilization in the Northern Hemisphere and the rise of the new civilization in South America and

ULLR UPRISING

South Africa and Australia. Today, the small-arms and artillery his troops were using were merely slight refinements on the weapons of the First Century, and all the modern nuclear weapons used by the Terran Federation were produced at the Space Navy base on Mars, by a small force of experts whose skills were almost as closed to the general scientific and technical world as the secrets of a medieval guild. The old A-bomb was an historical curiosity, and there was nobody on Ullr who had more than a layman's knowledge of the intricate technology of modern nuclear weapons. There were plenty of good nuclear-power engineers on Gongonk Island, but how long would it take them to design and build a plutonium bomb?

"... Gorkrink also has a good understanding of Lingua Terra," Paula was saying. "He and Dr. Murillo conversed bi-lingually, just as I've heard General von Schlichten and King Kankad talking to one another. I haven't any idea whether or not Gorkrink could read Lingua Terra, or, if so, what papers or plans he might have seen."

"Just a minute, Paula," he said. "Colonel Grinell, what does your branch have on this Gorkrink?"

"He's the son of King Orgzild, and the daughter of Prince Jurnkonk," Grinell said. "We knew he'd signed on for Nif, two years ago, but the story we got was that he'd fallen out of favor at court and had been exiled. I can see, now, that that was planted to mislead us. As to whether or not he can read Lingua Terra, my belief is that he can. We know that he can understand it when spoken. He could have learned to read at one of those schools Mohammed Ferriera set up, ten or fifteen years ago."

"And Dr. Gomes and Dr. Murillo and Dr. Livesey left papers and plans lying around all over the place," Paula added. "If he went to Niflheim as a spy, he could have copied almost anything."

"Well, there you have it," von Schlichten said. "When Gorkrink found out that plutonium can be used for bombs, he began gathering all the information he could. And as soon as he got home, he turned it all over to Pappy Orgzild."

"That still doesn't mean that the Kee-geeks were able to do anything with it," Air-Commodore Hargreaves argued.

"I think it does," von Schlichten differed. "As soon as Orgzild would hear about the possibility of making a plutonium bomb, he'd set up an A-bomb project, and don't think of it in terms of the old First Century Manhattan Project. There would be no problem of producing fissionables—we've been scattering refined plutonium over this planet like confetti."

"Well, an A-bomb's a pretty complicated piece of mechanism, even if you have the plans for it," Kent Pickering said. "As I recall, there have to be several subcritical masses of plutonium, or U-235, or whatever, blown together by shaped charges of explosive, all of which have to be fired simultaneously. That would mean a lot of electrical fittings that I can't see these geeks making by hand."

"I can," Paula said. "Have you ever seen the work these native jewelers do? And didn't you tell me about a clockwork thing they have at the university, here, to show the apparent movements of the sun...."

"That's right," von Schlichten said. "And what they couldn't make, they could have bought from us; we've sold them a lot of electrical equipment."

"All right, they could have built an A-bomb," Buhrmann said. "But did they?"

"We assume they tried to. Gorkrink got back from Nif on the *Canberra*, three months ago," von Schlichten said. "If Orgzild decided to build an A-bomb, he wouldn't give the signal for this uprising until he either had one or knew he couldn't make one, and he wouldn't give up trying in only three months. Therefore, I think we can assume that he succeeded, and had succeeded at the time he sent Gorkrink here to get that four tons of plutonium we let him have, and, incidentally, to tell his ambassador to pass the word to have Sid Harrington poisoned according to plan."

"Then why didn't he just use it on us at the start of the uprising?" Meyerstein wanted to know.

"Why should he? Getting rid of us is only the first step in Orgzild's plan," Grinell said. "Back as far as geek history goes, the Kings of Keegark have been trying to conquer Konkrook and the Free Cities and make themselves masters of the whole Takkad Sea area. Let Konkrook wipe us out, and then he can move in his troops and take Konkrook. Or, if we beat off the geeks here, as we seem to be doing, he can bomb us out and then move in on Konkrook. I think that as long as we're fighting, here, he'll wait. The more damage we do to Konkrook, the easier it'll be for him."

"Then we'd better start dragging our feet on the Konkrook front," Laviola said. "And get busy trying to build a bomb of our own."

*

Von Schlichten looked up at the big screen, on which the battle of Konkrook was being projected from an overhead pickup.

"I'll agree on the second half of it," von Schlichten said. "And we'll also have to set up some kind of security-patrol system against bombers from Keegark. And as soon as *Procyon* gets here, we'll have to send her out to hunt down and destroy those two Boer-class freighters, the *Jan Smuts* and the *Kruger*. And we'll have to arrange for protection of Kankad's Town; that's sure to be another of Orgzild's high-priority targets. As to the action against Konkrook, I'll rely on your advice, Them. Can we delay the fall of the city for any length of time?"

M'zangwe shook his head. "When we divert contragravity to security-patrol work, the ground action'll slow up a little, of course. But the geeks are about knocked out, now."

"The hell with it, then. I doubt if we'd be able to buy much time from Orgzild by delaying victory in the city, and we'll probably need the troops as workers over here." He turned to Pickering. "Dr. Pickering, what sort of a crew can you scrape together to design a bomb for us?" he asked.

"Well, there's Martirano, and Sternberg, and Howard Fu-Chung, and Piet van Reenen, and...." He nodded to himself. "I can get six or eight of them in here in about twenty minutes; I'll have a project set up and working in a couple of hours. There has to be somebody qualified on duty at the plant, all the time, of course, but...."

"All right; call them in. I want the bomb finished by yesterday afternoon. And everybody with you, and you, yourself, had better revert to civilian status. This isn't something you can do by the numbers, and I don't want anybody who doesn't know what it's all about pulling rank on your outfit. Go ahead, call in your gang, and let me know what you'll be able to do, as soon as—sooner than—it's possible."

He turned to Hargreaves. "Les, you'll have charge of flying the security patrols, and doing anything else you can to keep Orgzild from bombing us before we can bomb him. You'll have priority on everything second only to Pickering."

Hargreaves nodded. "As you say, general, we'll have to protect Kankad's, as well as this place. It's about five hundred miles from here to Kankad's, and eight-fifty miles from Kankad's to Keegark...."

*

He stopped talking to von Schlichten, and began muttering to himself, running over the names of ships, and the speeds and pay-load capacities of airboats, and distances. In about five minutes, he would have a program worked out; in the meantime, von Schlichten could only be patient and contain himself. He looked along the table, and caught sight of a thin-faced, saturnine-looking man in a green shirt with a colonel's three concentric circles marked on the shoulders in silver-paint. Emmett Pearson, the communications chief.

"Emmett," he said, "those orbiters you have strung around this planet, two thousand miles out, for telecast rebroadcast stations. How much of a crew could be put on one of them?"

Pearson laughed. "Crew of what, general? White mice, or trained cockroaches? There isn't room inside one of those things for anything bigger to move around."

"Well, I know they're automatic, but how do you service them?"

"From the outside. They're only ten feet through, by about twenty in length, with a fifteen-foot ball at either end, and everything's in sections, which can be taken out. Our maintenance-gang goes up in a thing like a small spaceship, and either works on the outside in spacesuits, or puts in a new section and brings the unserviceable one down here to the shops."

"Ah, and what sort of a thing is this small spaceship, now?"

"A thing like a pair of fifty-ton lorries, with airlocks between, and connected at the middle; airtight, of course, and pressurized and insulated, like a spaceship. One side's living' quarters for a six-man crew—sometimes the gang's out for as long as a week at a time—and the other side's a workshop."

That sounded interesting. With contragravity, of course, terms like "escape-velocity" and "mass-ratio" were of purely antiquarian interest.

"How long," he asked Pearson, "would it take to fit that vehicle with a full set of detection instruments—radar, infrared and ultraviolet vision, electron-telescope, heat and radiation detectors, the whole works—and spot it about a hundred to a hundred and fifty miles above Keegark?"

"That I couldn't say, general," Emmett Pearson replied. "It'd have to be a shipyard job, and a lot of that stuff's clear outside my department. Ask Air-Commodore Hargreaves."

"Les!" he called out. "Wake up, Les!"

"Just a second, general." Hargreaves scribbled frantically on his pad. "Now," he said, raising his head. "What is it, sir?"

"Emmett, here, has a junior-grade spaceship that he used to service those orbital telecast-relay stations of his. He'll tell you what it's like. I want it fitted with every sort of detection device that can be crammed into or onto it, and spotted above Keegark. It should, of course, be high enough to cover not only the Keegark area, but Konkrook, Kankad's, and the lower Hoork and Konk river-valleys."

"Yes, I get it." Hargreaves snatched up a phone, punched out a combination, and began talking rapidly into it in a low voice. After awhile, he hung up. "All right, Mr. Pearson—Colonel Pearson, I mean. Have your space-buggy sent around to the shipyard. My boys'll fix it up." He made a note on another piece of paper. "If we live through this, I'm going to have a couple of supra-atmosphere ships in service on this planet.... Now, general; I have a tentative set-up. We're going to need the *Elmoran* for patrol work south and east of Konkrook, and the *Gaucho* and *Bushranger* to the north and north-east, based on Kankad's. We'll keep the *Aldebaran* at Kankad's, and use her for emergencies. And we'll have patrols of light contragravity like this." He handed a map, with red-pencil and blue-pencil markings, along to von Schlichten. "Red are Kankad-based; blue are Konkrook-based."

"That looks all right," von Schlichten said. "There's another thing, though. We want scout-vehicles to cover the Keegark area with radiation-detectors. These geeks are quite well aware of radiation-danger from fissionables, but they're accustomed to the ordinary industrial-power reactors, which are either very lightly shielded or unshielded on top. We want to find out where Orgzild's bomb-plant is."

"Yes, general; as soon as we can get radiation detectors sent out to Kankad's, we'll have a couple of fast aircars fitted with them for that job."

"We have detectors, at our laboratory and reaction-plant," Kankad said. "And my people can make more, as soon as you want them." He thought for a moment. "Perhaps I should go to the town, now. I could be of more use there than here."

Kent Pickering, who had been talking with his experts at a table apart, returned.

"We've set up a program, general," he said. "It's going to be a lot harder than I'd anticipated. None of us seem to know exactly what we have to do in building one of those things. You see, the uranium or plutonium fission-bomb's been obsolete for over four hundred years. It was a classified-secret matter long after its obsolescence, because it hadn't been rendered any the less deadly by being superseded—there was that A-bomb that the Christian Anarchist Party put together at Buenos Aires in 378 A.E., for instance. And then, after it was declassified, it had been so far superseded that it was of only antiquarian interest; the textbooks dealt with it only in general terms. The principles, of course, are part of basic nuclear science; the secret of the A-bomb was just a bag of engineering tricks that we don't have, and which we will have to rediscover. Design of tampers, design of the chemical-explosive charges to bring subcritical masses together, case-design, detonating mechanism, things like that.

"The complete data on even the old Hiroshima and Nagasaki types is still in existence, of course. You can get it at places like the University of Montevideo Library, or Jan Smuts Memorial Library at Cape Town. But we don't have it here. We're detailing a couple of junior technicians to make a search of the library here on Gongonk Island, but we're not optimistic. We just can't afford to pass up any chance, even when it approaches zero-probability."

Von Schlichten nodded. "That's about what I'd expected," he said. "I suppose Gomes got his data out of one of the dustier storage-stacks at Jan Smuts or Montevideo, in the first place.... Well, I still want that bomb finished by yesterday afternoon, but since that's impractical, you'll have to take a little—but as little as possible—longer."

"What are we going to do about publicity on this?" Howlett, the personnel man. asked. "We don't want this getting out in garbled form—though how it could be made worse by garbling I couldn't guess—and having the troops watching the sky over their shoulders and going into a panic as soon as they saw something they didn't understand."

"No, we don't. I've seen a couple of troop-panics," von Schlichten said. "There can't be anything much worse than a panic."

"I think the Terrans ought to be told the worst," Hargreaves said. "And told that our only hope is to get a bomb of our own built and dropped first. As to the Kragans.... What do you think, King Kankad?"

"Tell them that we are building a bomb to destroy Keegark; that we are running short of ammunition, and that it is our only hope of finishing the war before the ammunition is gone," Kankad said. "Tell them something of what sort of a bomb it is. But do not tell them that King Orgzild already has such a bomb. Old Kankad, who made me out of himself, told me about how our people fled in panic from the weapons of the Terrans, when your people and mine were still enemies. This thing is to the weapons they faced then as those weapons were to the old Kragans' spears and bows.... And when the geeks from Grank come here, tell them that we are winning and that if they fight well, they can share the loot of Konkrook and Keegark."

Von Schlichten looked up at the big screen. Already, Themistocles M'zangwe had ordered the Channel Battery to reduce fire; the big guns were firing singly, in thirty-second-interval salvos. There was less bombing, too; contragravity was being drawn out of the battle.

"Well, we all have things to do," he said, "and I think we've discussed everything there is to discuss. Anybody think of anything we've forgotten?... Then we're adjourned."

He and Paula Quinton took the elevator to the roof, and sat side by side, silently watching the conflagration that was raging across the channel and the nearer flashes of the big guns along the island's city side.

"Wednesday night, I thought we were all cooked," Paula told him. "Cleaning up the North in two days seemed like an impossibility, too. Maybe you'll do it again."

"If I pull this one out of the fire, I won't be a general; I'll be a magician," he said. "Pickering'll be a magician, I mean; he's the boy who'll save our bacon, if it's saveable." He looked somberly across the flame-reflecting water. "Let's not kid ourselves; we're just kicking and biting at the guards on the way up the gallows-steps."

"Well, why stop till the trap's sprung?" she asked. "What'll happen to these people on this planet, after we're atomized?"

"That I don't want to think about. Kankad's Town will get the second bomb; Orgzild won't dare leave the Kragans after he's wiped us out.

Yoorkerk and Jonkvank, in the North, will turn on Keaveney and Shapiro and Karamessinis and Hid O'Leary and wipe them out. And when the next ship gets in here and they find out what happened, they'll send the Federation Space Navy, and this planet'll get it worse than Fenris did. They'll blast anything that has four arms and a face like a lizard...."

Half a dozen aircars lifted suddenly from the airport and streaked away to the north-east. As they went past, in the light of the burning-city, he could see that at least three of them had multiple rocket-launchers on top. In a matter of seconds, a gun-cutter raced after them, and a second, which had been over Konkrook, jettisoned a bomb and turned away to follow.

"Maybe that's it," Paula said.

"Well, if it is, we won't be any better off anywhere else than here," he told her. "Let's stay where we are and watch."

After what seemed like a long time, however, a twinkle of lights showed over the East Konk Mountains. They weren't the flashes of explosions; some were magnesium flares, and some were the lights of a ship.

"That's *Procyon*, from Grank," he said. "Everybody gets a good mark for this—detection stations, interceptors, gun-cutters. If that had been it, there'd have been a good chance of stopping it." He felt better than he had since Pickering had told him that Lourenço Gomes was dead. "It's a good thing Gorkrink didn't pick up any dope on guided missiles, while he was at it. As long as they have to deliver it with contragravity, we have a chance."

They rose from the balustrade where they had been sitting, and, for the first time, he discovered that he had had his left arm over her shoulder and that she had had her right hand resting on the point of his right hip, just above his pistol. He picked up the folder of papers she had been carrying, and put her into the elevator ahead of him, and it was only when they parted on the living-quarters level that he recalled having followed the older protocol of gallantry rather than the precedence of military rank.

XII

He woke with a guilty start and looked up at the clock on the ceiling; it was 0945. Kicking himself free of the covers, he slid his feet to the floor and sprinted for the bathroom. While he was fussing to get the shower adjusted to the right temperature, he bludgeoned his conscience by telling himself that a wide-awake general is more good than a half-asleep general, that there was nothing he could do but hope that Hargreaves' patrols would keep the bomb away from Konkrook until Pickering's brain-trust came up with one of their own, and that the fact that the commander-in-chief was making sack-time would be much better for morale than the spectacle of him running around in circles. He shaved carefully; a stubble of beard on his chin might betray the fact that he was worried. Then he dressed, put his monocle in his eye, and called the headquarters that had been set up in Sid Harrington's—now his—office. A girl at the switchboard appeared on his screen, and gave place to Paula Quinton, who had been up for the past two hours.

"The *Northern Lights* got in about three hours ago, general," she told him. "She had four of King Yoorkerk's infantry regiments aboard—the Seventh, Glorious-and-Terrible, the Fourth, Firm-in-Adversity, the Second, Strength-of-the-Throne, and the Twelfth, Forever-Admirable. They're the sorriest looking rabble I ever saw, but Hideyoshi says they're the best Yoorkerk has, and they all have Terran-style rifles. General M'zangwe broke them into battalions, and put a battalion in with each of the Kragan regiments. I think they're more afraid of the Kragans than they are of the rebels."

He nodded. That was probably the best way to employ them, within the existing situation. The trouble was, Them M'zangwe was incurably tactical-minded. Put those geeks of Yoorkerk's in with the Kragans and they'd be most useful in conquering Konkrook, but the trouble was that, after associating with Kragans, they might develop into reasonably good troops, themselves, to the undesired improvement of King Yoorkerk's army. On the other hand, maybe not. Keep them in Company service long enough, and they might want to forget about Yoorkerk and stay there.

"How's the situation over in town?" he asked.

"Well, it's slowing up, since we began pulling contragravity out," she told him, "but the geeks are breaking up rapidly.... Oh, there was something funny about that hassle, last evening, when the Procyon came in. Two contragravity vehicles, an aircar and an air-lorry, that went out to meet the ship, are unaccounted for."

"You mean two of our vehicles are missing?"

She shook her head, frowning in perplexity. "Well, no. All the vehicles that answered that unidentified-aircraft alert returned, but there were these two that went out that we haven't any record of. Colonel Grinell is investigating, but he can't find out anything...."

"Tell him not to waste any more time," he said. "Those two were probably geeks from Konkrook. You know, that's how the von Schlichten family got out of Germany, in the Year Three—flew a bomber to Spain. The Konkrook war-criminals are getting out before the Army of Occupation moves in."

"Well, the posts at the old Kragan castles report some contragravity, and parties riding 'saurs, moving west from the city," she told him. "There are a lot of refugees on the roads. And combat reports from Konkrook agree that resistance is getting weaker every hour.... And the supra-atmosphere observation-craft—they're beginning to call her the Sky-Spy—is up a hundred and fifty miles over Keegark. We have radar and vision screens and telemetered radiation and other detectors here, tuned to her. They're installing a similar set on the *Northern Lights* at the shipyard. By the way, Air-Commodore Hargreaves wants to know if he can take a pair of 155-mm rifles from the Channel Battery and mount them on the *Lights*."

"Yes, of course; he can have anything he wants, as long as it isn't urgently needed for the bomb project."

"*Sky-Spy* reports normal contragravity traffic between Keegark and the farming-villages around—aircars, lorries, a few scows—but nothing suspicious. No trace of either of the Boer-class ships. Kankad's people are building receiving sets to install on the *Procyon* and the *Aldebaran*, and another set for Kankad's Town. Pickering and his people are still working, but they all look pretty frustrated. They have Major Thornton, at the ammunition plant, doing experimental work on chemical-explosive charges to bring the subcritical masses together and hold them together till an explosion can be produced; they're using most of the skilled electrical and electronics people to work up a detonating device. That's why Kankad's people are doing most of the detection-device work. Hargreaves is fitting a lot of small craft—combat-cars and civilian aircars—with radar sets, to use for patrolling."

"That sounds good," von Schlichten said. "I'll be around and see how things are, after I've had some breakfast."

He had breakfast at the main cafeteria, four floors down; there wasn't as much laughing and talking as usual, but the crowd there seemed in good spirits. He spent some time at headquarters, watching Keegark by TV and radar. So far, nothing had been done about direct reconnaissance over Keegark with radiation-detectors, but Hargreaves reported that a couple of privately-owned aircars were being fitted for the job.

He made a flying inspection trip around the island, and visited the farms south of the city, on the mainland, and, finally, made a sweep in his command-car over the city itself. Reconnaissance in person was an archaic and unprogressive procedure, and it was a good way to get generals killed, but one could see a lot of things that would be missed on TV. He let down several times in areas that had already been taken, and talked to company and platoon officers. For one thing, King Yoorkerk's flamboyantly-named regiments weren't quite as bad as Paula had thought. She'd been spoiled by the Kragans in her appreciation of other native troops. They had good, standard-quality, Volund-made arms; they were brave and capable; and they had been just enough insulted by being integrated into Kragan regiments to try to make a good showing.

By noon, resistance in the city was beginning to cave in. Surrender flags were appearing on one after another of the Konkrookan rebel strong-points, and at 1430, after he had returned to the Island, a delegation, headed by the Konkrookan equivalent of Lord Mayor and composed largely of prominent merchants, came across the channel under a flag of truce to surrender the city's Spear of State, with abject apologies for not having Gurgurk's head on the point of it. Gurgurk, they reported had fled to Keegark by air the night before, which explained the incident of the unaccountable aircar and lorry. The Channel Battery stopped firing, and, with the exception of an occasional spatter of small-arms fire, the city fell silent.

At 1600, von Schlichten visited the headquarters Pickering had set up in the office building at the power-plant. As he stepped off the lift on the third floor, a girl, running down the hall with her arms full of papers in folders, collided with him; the load of papers flew in all directions. He stooped to help her pick them up.

"Oh, general! Isn't it wonderful?" she cried. "I just can't believe it!"

"Isn't what wonderful?" he asked.

"Oh, don't you know? They've got it!"

"Huh? They have?" He gathered up the last of the big envelopes and gave them to her. "When?"

"Just half an hour ago. And to think, those books were around here all the time, and.... Oh, I've got to run!" She disappeared into the lift.

Inside the office, one of Pickering's engineers was sitting on the middle of his spinal column, a stenograph-phone in one hand and a book in the other. Once in a while, he would say something into the mouthpiece of the phone. Two other nuclear engineers had similar books spread out on a desk in front of them; they were making notes and looking up references in the Nuclear Engineers' Handbook, and making calculations with their slide-rules. There was a huddle around the drafting-boards, where two more such books were in use.

"Well, what's happened?" he demanded, catching Pickering by the arm as he rushed from one group to another.

"Ha! We have it!" Pickering cried. "Everything we need! Look!"

He had another of the books under his arm. He held it out to von Schlichten, and von Schlichten suddenly felt sicker than he had ever felt since, at the age of fourteen, he had gotten drunk for the first time. He had seen men crack up under intolerable strain before, but this was the first time he had seen a whole roomful of men blow their tops in the same manner.

The book was a novel—a jumbo-size historical novel, of some seven or eight hundred pages. Its dust-jacket bore a slightly-more-than-bust-length picture of a young lady with crimson hair and green eyes and jade earrings and a plunging—not to say power-diving—neckline that left her affiliation with the class of Mammalia in no doubt whatever. In the background, a mushroom-topped smoke-column rose, and away from it something intended to be a four-motor propeller-driven bomber of the First Century was racing madly. The title, he saw, was *Dire Dawn*, and the author was one Hildegarde Hernandez.

"Well, it has a picture of an A-bomb explosion an it," he agreed.

"It has more than that; it has the whole business. Case specifications, tampers, charge design, detonating device, everything. Why, end-papers even have diagrams: copies of the original Nagasaki-bomb drawing. Look."

Von Schlichten looked. He had no more than the average intelligent layman's knowledge of nuclear physics—enough to recharge or repair a conversion-unit—but the drawings looked authentic enough. They seemed to be copies of ancient blueprints, lettered in First Century English, with Lingua Terra translations added, and marked TOP SECRET and U. S. ARMY CORPS OF ENGINEERS and MANHATTAN ENGINEERING DISTRICT.

"And look at this!" Pickering opened at a marked page and showed it to him. "And this!" He opened where another slip of paper had been inserted. "Everything we want to know, practically."

"I don't get this." He wasn't sick, any more; just bewildered. "I read some reviews of this thing. All the reviewers panned hell out of it—'World War II Through a Bedroom Keyhole'; 'Henty in Black Lace Panties'—that sort of thing."

"Yeh, yeh, sure," Pickering agreed. "But this Hernandez has illusions of being a great serious historical novelist, see. She won't try to write a book till she's put in years of research—actually, about six months' research by a herd of librarians and college-juniors and other such literary coolies—and she boasts that she never yet has been caught in an error of historical background detail.

"Well, this opus is about the old Manhattan Project. The heroine is a sort of super-Mata-Hari, who is, alternately and sometimes simultaneously, in the pay of the Nazis, the Soviets, the Vatican, Chiang Kai-Shek, the Japanese Emperor, and the Jewish International Bankers, and she has affairs with everybody from Joe Stalin to Joe McCarthy, and of course, she is in on every step of the A-bomb project. She even manages to stow away on the Enola Gay, with the help of a general she's spent fifty incandescent pages seducing.

"In order to tool up for this production-job, La Hernandez did her researching just where Lourenço Gomes probably did his—University of Montevideo Library. She even had access to the photostats of the old U. S. data that General Lanningham brought to South America after the debacle in the United States in A.E. 114. Those end-papers are part of the Lanningham stuff. As far as we've been able to check mathematically, everything is strictly authentic and practical. We'll have to run a few more tests on the chemical-explosive charges—we don't have any data on the exact strength of the explosives they used then—and the tampers and detonating device will need to be tested a little. But in about half an hour, we ought to be able to start drawing plans for the case, and as soon as they're finished, we'll rush them to the shipyard foundries for casting."

Von Schlichten handed the book back to Pickering, and sighed deeply. "And I thought everybody here had gone off his rocker," he said. "We will erect, on the ruins of Keegark, a hundred-foot statue of Señorita Hildegrade Hernandez.... How did you get onto this?"

Pickering pointed to a young man with dull brick colored hair, who was punching out some kind of a problem on a small computing machine.

"Piet van Reenen, over there; he has a girl-friend whose taste runs to this sort of literary bubble-gum. She told him it was all in a book she'd just read, and showed him. We descended in force on the bookshop and grabbed every copy in stock. We are now running a sort of gaseous-diffusion process, to separate the nuclear physics from the pornography. I must say, Hildegarde has her biological data very well in hand, too."

"I'll bet she'd have fun writing a novel about these geeks," von Schlichten said. "Well, how soon do you think you can have a bomb made up and all ready for us?"

"Casting the cases is going to slow us down the most," Pickering said. "But, even with that, we ought to have one ready in three days, at the most. By two weeks, we'll be turning them out on an assembly-line."

"I hope we don't need more than one. But you'd better produce at least half a dozen. And have some practice-bombs made up, out of concrete or anything, as long as they're the right weight and airfoil and have some way of releasing smoke. Get them done as soon as you have your case designed. We want to be able to make a couple of practice drops."

There was no use, he thought, of raising hopes which might prove premature. He told Paula Quinton, of course, and Themistocles M'zangwe, and, by telecast on sealed beam, King Kankad and Air-Commodore Hargreaves. Beyond that, there was nothing to do but wait, and hope that Hargreaves could keep Orgzild's bombers away from Gongonk Island and Kankad's Town and that Hildegarde Hernandez had been playing fair with her public. He visited the city, where a few pockets of die-hard resistance were being liquidated, and where everybody who had not been too deeply and publicly involved in the *znidd suddabit* conspiracy was now coming forward and claiming to have been a lifelong friend of the Terrans and the Company. Von Schlichten returned to Gongonk Island, debating with himself whether to declare a general amnesty or to set up a dozen guillotines in the city and run them around the clock for a week. There were cogent arguments for and against either procedure.

By 2100, the last organized resistance had been wiped out, a curfew had been imposed, and peace of a sort restored. There was still the threat from Keegark, but it was looking less ominous now than it had the evening before. Von Schlichten and Paula were having dinner in the Broadway Room, confident that there was nothing left to do that they could do anything about, when the extension phone that had been plugged in at their table rang.

"Colonel Quinton here," Paula identified herself into it, and listened for a moment. "There has? When?... Well, where did it come from?... I see. And the direction?... Anything else?"

Apparently there was nothing else. She hung up, and turned to von Schlichten.

"The *Sky-Spy* just detected a ship lifting out from Keegark, presumed one of the Boer-class freighters, either the *Jan Smuts* or the *Oom Paul Kruger*. It was first picked up on contragravity at about a hundred feet, rising vertically from near the Palace. The supposition is the geeks had her camouflaged since the time Commander Prinsloo first bombarded Keegark with the *Aldebaran*. That was about twenty minutes ago; at last report, she's fifty miles north of Keegark, headed up the Hoork River."

Von Schlichten started thinking aloud: "That could be a feint, to draw our ships north after her, and leave the approach to Konkrook or Kankad's open, but that would be presuming that they know about the *Sky-Spy*, and I doubt that, though not enough to take chances on. They know we have ground and ship-radar, and they may think they can slip down the Konk Valley either undetected or mistaken for one of our ships from North Ullr."

He picked up the phone. "Get me through on telecast to Air-Commodore Hargreaves, aboard the *Procyon*," he said. "I'll take it in the office; I'll be up directly." He rose. "Finish your dinner, and have the rest of mine sent up," he told Paula.

Leaving the elevator, he rushed into the big headquarters room just as contact was established with the *Procyon*, on station over the north-western corner of Takkad Sea, between Kankad's Town and Keegark. The

Aldebaran, he knew, was west of Keegark; the *Northern Lights*, now fitted with a pair of 155-mm guns, in addition to her 90's, had just arrived at Kankad's. He had the *Aldebaran* sent north along the crest of the mountain-range between the Hoork and Konk river-valleys, where she could cover both with her own radar and other detection-devices and exchange information with the *Sky-Spy*, and the *Gaucho* sent in what looked like the right course to intercept the Boer-class freighter from Keegark. The *Northern Lights*, also with screens tuned to the *Sky-Spy*, was sent to take over the Aldebaran's regular station. Finally, he called Skilk and had the *Northern Star* sent south down the Hoork Valley.

After that, there was nothing to do but wait, and watch the screens. Paula Quinton put in an appearance shortly after he had finished calling Skilk, pushing a cocktail-wagon on which their interrupted dinners had been placed. They finished eating, and drank coffee, and smoked. Most of the rest of his staff who were not busy on the bomb-project or at the shipyards or with the occupation of Konkrook drifted in; they all sat and stared from one to another of the screens, which told, in radar-patterns and direct vision and telescopic vision and heat and radiation detection, the story of what was going on to the north-east of them.

Keegark was dark, on the vision-screen; evidently King Orgzild had invented the blackout, too. Not that it did him any good; the radar-screen showed the city clearly, and it was just as clear on the radiation and heat screens. The Keegarkan ship was completely blacked out, but the radiations from her engines and the distinctive radiation-pattern of her contragravity-field showed clearly, and there was a speck that marked her position on the radar-screen. The same position was marked with a pin-point of light on the vision screen—some device on *Sky-Spy*, synchronized with the detectors, kept it focused there. The Company ships and contragravity vehicles all were carrying topside lights, visible only from above, which flashed alternate red and blue to identify them.

Time crawled slowly around the clock-face on the wall, the sixty-five-second minutes of Ullr dragging like hours. The spots that marked the enemy ship and her hunters crawled, too; seen from the hundred-and-fifty-mile altitude of the *Sky-Spy*, even the six-hundred-mile speed of the *Gaucho* was barely visible. They drank coffee till the stuff revolted them; they smoked until their throats and mouths were dry, they watched the screens until they thought that they would see them in their dreams forever. Then the *Gaucho* reported radar-contact with the Keegarkan ship, which had begun to turn in a hairpin-shaped course and was coming south down the Konk Valley.

After that, the *Gaucho* began reporting directly, and her topside identification-light went out.

"... doused our lights; we're down in the valley, altitude about a thousand feet. We're trying to get a glimpse of her against the sky," a voice came in. "We're cutting in our forward TV-pick-up." The voice repeated, several times, the wavelength, and somebody got an auxiliary screen tuned in. There was nothing visible in it but the darkness of the valley, the star-jeweled sky, and the loom of the East Konk Mountains. "We still can't see her, but we ought to, any moment; radar shows her well above the mountains. Ah, there she is; she just obscured Beta Hydrae V; she's moving toward that big constellation to the east of it, the one they call Finnegan's Goat. Now she'll be right in the center of the screen; we're going straight for her. We're going to try to slow her down till *Aldebaran* can get here...."

The enemy ship was vaguely visible, now, becoming clearer in the starlight. She was a Boer-class freighter, all right. Probably the *Jan Smuts*; the *Oom Paul Kruger* had last been reported at Bwork, and there was little chance that she had slipped into Keegark since the uprising had started. For all anybody knew, she could have been destroyed in the fighting before the Bwork Residency fell.

"All right, we have her spotted; we're going to open up on her," the voice from the *Gaucho* announced. "She has two 90's to our one; we'll try to disable them, first." The vision-screen lit with the indirect glare of the gun-flash, and the image in it jiggled violently as the ship shook to the recoil, then steadied again, with the enemy ship visible in the middle of it, growing larger and larger as the *Gaucho* rushed toward her. The gun fired again and again, flooding the screen with momentary yellow light and disturbing the image as the recoil shook the gun-cutter. The enemy ship began firing in reply; the shots were all wide misses. Apparently the geek gun-crew didn't know how to synchronize the radar sights, and were ignorant of the correct setting for the proximity-fuzes. The *Gaucho's* searchlights came on, bathing her quarry in light. It was the *Jan Smuts*; the name, and the figure-head-bust of the old soldier-philosopher, were plainly visible. Her forward gun had been knocked out, and she was trying to swing about to get a field of fire for her stern-gun.

"We're going to give her a rocket-salvo," the voice said. "Watch this, now!"

The rockets leaped forward, from the topside racks, four and four and four and four, at half-second intervals. The first four hit the Smuts amidships and low, exploding with a flare that grew before it could die away as the second four landed. Nobody ever saw the third and fourth four land. The Jan Smuts vanished in a blaze of light that blinded everybody in the room; when they could see again, after some thirty seconds, the screen was dark.

In the direct-vision screen from the Sky-Spy, the whole countryside of the Konk Valley, five hundred miles north of Konkrook, was lighted. The heat and radiation detectors were going insane. And in the shifting confusion on the radar-screen, there was no trace either of the Jan Smuts or the Gaucho.

"Well, the geeks did have an A-bomb," Themistocles M'zangwe said, at length. "I'd been trying to kid myself that we were just preparing against a million-to-one chance. I wonder how many more they have."

"Paula, find out who was in command of the Gaucho; he'd be a junior-grade lieutenant. Fix up orders promoting him to navy captain, as of now. It's probably the only thing we can do for him, any more. And promotions of the same order for everybody else aboard that cutter. Authority Carlos von Schlichten, acting Governor-General." He picked up a phone. "Get me Commander Prinsloo, on Aldebaran...."

He ordered Prinsloo to launch airboats and make a search; cautioned him to be careful of radiation, but to take no chances on any of the Gaucho's complement being still alive and in need of help. While that was going on, the Sky-Spy reported another ship coming over her horizon to the east, from the direction of Bwork. That would be the Oom Paul Kruger. Hargreaves had already learned of the advent of the second freighter. He was unwilling to take the Procyon off her station until the Aldebaran returned from the Konk Valley. In this, von Schlichten concurred.

Somebody suggested that a drink would be in order. They had just watched the all-but-certain death of three Terran officers, fifteen Terran airmen, and ten Kragans, but they had all been living in too close companionship with death in the past three days—or was it three centuries—to be too deeply affected. And they had also watched, at least for a day or so, the removal of the threat that had hung over their heads. And they had seen proof that they had a defense against King Orgzild's bombs.

They were still mixing cocktails when Pickering phoned in.

"Some good news, general, from Operation 'Hildegarde.' We ought to have at least one bomb ready to drop by 1500 tomorrow; four or five more by next mid-night," he said. "We don't need to have cases cast. We got our dimensions decided, and we find that there are a lot of big empty liquid-oxygen flasks, or tanks, rather, at the spaceport, that'll accommodate everything—fissionables, explosive-charges, tampers, detonator, and all."

"Well, go ahead with it. Make up a few of them; as many as you can between now and 2400 Sunday." He thought for a moment. "Don't waste time on those practice bombs I mentioned. We'll make a practice drop with a live bomb. And don't throw away the design for the cast case. We may need that, later on."

XIII

The Company fleet hung off Keegark, at fifteen thousand feet, in a belt of calm air just below the seesawing currents from the warming Antarctic and the cooling deserts of the Arctic. There was the *Procyon*, from the bridge of which von Schlichten watched the movements of the other ships and airboats and the distant horizon. The *Aldebaran* was ten miles off, to the west, her metal sheathing glinting the red light of the evening sun. There was the *Northern Star*, down from Skilk, a smaller and more distant twinkle of reflected light to the north of *Aldebaran*. The *Northern Lights* was off to the east, and between her and *Procyon* was a fifth ship; turning the arm-mounted binoculars around, he could just make out, on her bow, the figure-head bust of a man in an ancient top-hat and a fringe of chin-beard. She was the *Oom Paul Kruger*, captured by the *Procyon* after a chase across the mountains north-east of Keegark the day before. And, remote from the other ships, to the south, a tiny speck of blue-gray, almost invisible against the sky, and a smaller twinkle of reflected sunlight—a garbage-scow, unflatteringly but somewhat aptly rechristened *Hildegarde Hernandez*, which had been altered as a bomb-carrier, and the gun-cutter *Elmoran*. With the glasses, he could see a bulky cylinder being handled off the scow and loaded onto the improvised bomb-catapult on the *Elmoran's* stern. Shortly thereafter, the gun-cutter broke loose from the tender and began to approach the fleet.

"General, I must protest again against your doing this," Air-Commodore Hargreaves said. "There's simply no sense in it. That bomb can be dropped without your personal supervision aboard, sir, and you're endangering yourself unnecessarily. That infernal-machine hasn't been tested or anything; it might even let go on the catapult when you try to drop it. And we simply can't afford to lose you, now."

"No, what would become of us, if you go out there and blow yourself up with that contraption?" Buhrmann supported him. "My God, I thought Don Quixote was a Spaniard, instead of a German!"

"Argentino," von Schlichten corrected. "And don't try to sell me that Irreplaceable-Man, either. Them M'zangwe can replace me, Hid O'Leary can replace him, Barney Mordkovitz can replace him, and so on down to where you make a second lieutenant out of some sergeant. We've been all over this last evening. Admitted we can't take time for a long string of test-shots, and admitted we have to use an untested weapon; I'm not sending men out under those circumstances and staying here on this ship and watch them blow themselves up. If that bomb's our only hope, it's got to be dropped right, and I'm not going to take a chance on having it dropped by a crew who think they've been sent out on a suicide mission. What happened to the *Gaucho* when she blew the *Smuts* up is too fresh in everybody's mind. But if I, who ordered the mission, accompany it, they'll know I have some confidence that they'll come back alive."

*

"Well, I'm coming along, too, general," Kent Pickering spoke up. "I made the damned thing, and I ought to be along when it's dropped, on the principle that a restaurant-proprietor ought to be seen eating his own food once in a while."

"I still don't see why we couldn't have made at least one test shot, first," Hans Meyerstein, the Banking Cartel man, objected.

"Well, I'll tell you why," Paula Quinton spoke up. "There's a good chance that the geeks don't know we have a bomb of our own. They may believe that it was something invented on Niflheim for mining purposes, and that we haven't realized its military application. There's more than a good chance that the loss of the *Jan Smuts* has temporarily demoralized them. Personally, I believe that both King Orgzild and Prince Gorkrink were aboard her when she blew up. That's something we'll never know, positively, of course. That ship and everything and everybody in her were simply vaporized, and the particles are registering on our geigers now. But I'm as sure as I am of anything about these geeks that one or both of them accompanied her."

"Paula knows what she's talking about," King Kankad jabbered in the Takkad Sea language which they all understood. "Just like Von saying that he has to go on our cutter, to encourage the crew. They always insist that their kings and generals go into battle, particularly if something important is to be done. They think the gods get angry if they don't."

"And we have to hit them now," von Schlichten said. "They still have a couple of bombs left. We haven't been able to locate them with detectors, but those geeks Kankad's men caught on that commando-raid, last night, say that there were at least three of them made. We can't take a chance that some fanatic may load one into an aircar and make a kamikaze-raid on Gongonk Island."

*

The *Elmoran* ran alongside, with her Masai-warrior figure-head and the black cylinder on her catapult aft. Somebody had painted, on the bomb: DIRE DAWN *by Hildegarde Hernandez. Compliments of the author to H. M. King Orgzild of Keegark.* A canvas-entubed gangway was run out to connect the ship with the cutter. Von Schlichten and Kent Pickering went down the ladder from the bridge, the others accompanying them. As he stepped into the gangway, Paula Quinton fell in behind him.

"Where do you think you're going?" he demanded.

"Along with you," she replied. "I'm your adjutant, I believe."

"You definitely are not going along. Personally, I don't believe there's any danger, but I'm not having you run any unnecessary risks...."

"Von, I don't know much about the way Terrans think, except about fighting and about making things," Kankad told him. "And I don't know anything at all about the kind of Terrans who have young. But I believe this is something important to Paula. Let her go with you, because if you go alone and don't come back I don't think she will ever be happy again."

He looked at Kankad curiously, wondering, as he had so often before, just what went on inside that lizard-skull. Then he looked at Paula, and, after a moment, he nodded.

"All right, colonel; objection withdrawn," he said.

Aboard the *Elmoran*, they gave the bomb a last-minute inspection and checked the catapult and the bomb-sight, and then went up on the bridge.

"Ready for the bombing mission, sir?" the skipper, a Lieutenant (j.g.) Morrison, asked.

"Ready if you are, Lieutenant. Carry on; we're just passengers."

"Thank you, sir. We'd thought of going in over the city at about five thousand for a target-check, turning when we're half way back to the mountains, and coming back for our bombing-run at fifteen thousand. Is that all right, sir?"

Von Schlichten nodded. "You're the skipper, lieutenant. You'd better make sure, though, that as soon as the bomb-off signal is flashed, your engineer hits his auxiliary rocket-propulsion button. We want to be about fifteen miles from where that thing goes off."

The lieutenant (j.g.) muttered something that sounded unmilitarily like, "You ain't foolin', brother!"

"No, I'm not," von Schlichten agreed. "I saw the *Jan Smuts* on the TV-screen."

*

The *Elmoran* pointed her bow, and the long blade of the figure-head warrior's spear, toward Keegark. The city grew out of the ground-mist, a particolored blur at the delta of the dry Hoork River, and then a color-splashed triangle between the river and the bay and the hills on the landward side, and then it took shape, cross-ruled with streets and granulated with buildings. As they came in, von Schlichten, who had approached it from the air many times before, could distinguish the landmarks—the site of King Orgzild's nitroglycerine plant, now a crater surrounded by a quarter-mile radius of ruins; the Residency, another crater since Rodolfo MacKinnon had blown it up under him; the smashed *Christian De Wett* at the Company docks; King Orgzild's palace, fire-stained and with a hole blown in one corner by the *Aldebaran's* bombs.... Then they were past the city and over open country.

"I wish we had some idea where the rest of those bombs are stored, sir," Lieutenant Morrison said. "We don't seem to have gotten anything significant when we flew reconnaissance with the radiation detectors."

"No; about all that was picked up was the main power-plant, and the radiation-escape from there was normal," Pickering agreed. "The bombs themselves wouldn't be detectable, except to the extent that, say, a nuclear-conversion engine for an airboat would be. They probably have them underground, somewhere, well shielded."

"Those prisoners Kankad's commandos dragged in only knew that they were in the city somewhere," von Schlichten considered. "How about midway between the Palace and the Residency for our ground-zero, lieutenant? That looks like the center of the city."

The cutter turned and started back, having risen another ten thousand feet. Morrison passed the word to the bombardier. The city, with the sea beyond it now, came rushing at them, and von Schlichten, standing at the front of the bridge, discovered that he had his arm around Paula's waist and was holding her a little more closely than was military. He made no attempt to release her, however.

"There's nothing to worry about, really," he was assuring her. "Pickering's boys built this thing according to the best principles of engineering, and the stuff they got out of that big-economy-size shilling-shocker all checked mathematically...."

The red light on the bridge flashed, and the intercom shouted "*Bomb off!*" He forced Paula down on the bridge deck and crouched beside her.

"Cover your eyes," he warned. "You remember what the flash was like in the screen, when the *Jon Smuts* blew up. And we didn't get the worst of it; the pickup on the *Gaucho* was knocked out too soon."

He kept on lecturing her about gamma-rays and ultraviolet rays and X-rays and cosmic rays, trying to keep making some sort of intelligent sounds while they clung together and waited, and, with the other half of his mind, trying not to think of everything that could go wrong with that jerry-built improvisation they had just dumped onto Keegark. If it didn't blow, and the geeks found it, they'd know that another one would be along shortly, and....

*

An invisible hand caught the gun-cutter and hurled her end-over-end, sending von Schlichten and Paula sprawling at full length on the deck, still clinging to one another. There was a blast of almost palpable sound, and a sensation of heat that penetrated even the airtight superstructure of the *Elmoran*. An instant later, there was another, and another, similar shock. Two more bombs had gone off behind them, in Keegark; that meant that they had found King Orgzild's remaining nuclear armament. There were shattering sounds of breaking glass, and heavy thumps that told of structural damage to the cutter, and hoarse shouts, and lurid cursing as Morrison and his airmen struggled with the controls. The cutter began losing altitude, but she was back on a reasonably even keel. Von Schlichten rose, helping Paula to her feet, and found that they had been kissing one another passionately. They were still in each other's arms when the pitching and rolling of the cutter ceased and somebody tapped him on the shoulder.

He came out of the embrace and looked around. It was Lieutenant (j.g.) Morrison.

"What the devil, lieutenant?" he demanded.

"Sorry to interrupt, sir, but we're starting back to *Procyon*. And here; you'll want this, I suppose." He held out a glass disc. "I never expected to see it, but at that it took three A-bombs to blow you loose from your monocle."

"Oh, that?" Von Schlichten took his trade mark and set it in his eye. "I didn't lose it," he lied. "I just jettisoned it. Don't you know, lieutenant, that no gentleman ever wears a monocle while he's kissing a lady?"

He looked around. They were at about eight hundred to a thousand feet above the water, with a stiff following wind away from the explosion area. The 90-mm gun, forward, must have been knocked loose and carried away; it was gone, and so was the TV-pickup and the radar. Something, probably the gun, had slammed against the front of the bridge—the metal skeleton was bent in, and the armor-glass had been knocked out. The cutter was vibrating properly, so the contragravity-field had not been disturbed, and her jets were firing.

"It was the second and third bombs that did the damage, sir," Morrison was saying. "We'd have gone through the effects of our own bomb with nothing more than a bad shaking—of course, on contragravity, we're weightless relative to the air-mass, but she was built to stand the winds in the high latitudes. But the two geek bombs caught us off balance...."

"You don't need to apologize, lieutenant. You and your crew behaved splendidly, lieutenant-commander; best traditions, and all that sort of thing. It was a pleasure, commander; hope to be aboard with you again, captain."

They found Kent Pickering at the rear of the bridge, and joined him, looking astern. Even von Schlichten, who had seen H-bombs and Bethe-cycle bombs, was impressed. Keegark was completely obliterated under an outward-rolling cloud of smoke and dust that spread out for five miles at the bottom of the towering column.

*

There had been a hundred and fifty thousand people in that city, even if their faces were the faces of lizards and they had four arms and quartz-speckled skins. What fraction of them were now alive, he could not guess. He had to remind himself that they were the people who had burned Eric Blount and Hendrik Lemoyne alive; that two of the three bombs that had contributed to that column of boiling smoke had been made in Keegark, by Keegarkans, and that, with a few casual factors altered, he was seeing what would have happened to Konkrook. Perhaps every Terran felt a superstitious dread of nuclear energy turned to the purposes of war; small wonder, after what they had done on their own world.

For one thing, he thought grimly, the next geek who picks up the idea of soaking a Terran in thermoconcentrate and setting fire to him will drop it again like a hot potato. And the next geek potentate who tries to organize an anti-Terran conspiracy, or the next crazy caravan-driver who preaches *znidd suddabit*, will be lynched on the spot. But this must be the last nuclear bomb used on Ullr....

Drunkard's morning-after resolution! he told himself contemptuously. The next time, it will come easier, and easier still the time after that. After you drop the first bomb, there is no turning back, any more than there had been after Hiroshima, four-hundred-and-fifty-odd years ago. Why, he had even been considering just where, against the mountains back of Bwork, he would drop a demonstration bomb as a prelude to a surrender demand.

You either went on to the inevitable catastrophe, or you realized, in time, that nuclear armament and nationalism cannot exist together on the same planet, and it is easier to banish a habit of thought than a piece of knowledge. Ullr was not ready for membership in the Terran Federation; then its people must bow to the Terran Pax. The Kragans would help—as proconsuls, administrators, now, instead of mercenaries. And there must be manned orbital stations, and the Residencies must be moved outside the cities, away from possible blast-areas. And Sid Harrington's idea of encouraging the natives to own their contragravity-ships must be shelved, for a long time to come. Maybe, in time....

Kankad had a good idea, at that; a most meritorious idea. He was sold on it, already, and he doubted if it would take much salesmanship with Paula, either. Already, she was clinging to his arm with obvious possessiveness. Maybe their grandchildren, and the Kankad of that time, would see Ullr a civilized member of the Federation....

They paused, as the gun-cutter nuzzled up to the *Procyon* and the canvas-entubed gangway was run out and made fast, looking back at the fearful thing that had sprouted from where Keegark had been.

"You know," Paula was saying, echoing his earlier thought, "but for the female pornographer, that would have been Konkrook."

He nodded. "Yes. I hope you won't mind, but there will always be a place in my heart for Hildegarde."

Then they turned their backs upon the abomination of Keegark's desolation and went up the gangway together, looking very little like a general and his adjutant.